KRISTINE ROLOFSON

MADE IN TEXAS

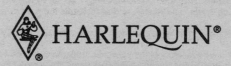

HARLEQUIN®

TORONTO • NEW YORK • LONDON
AMSTERDAM • PARIS • SYDNEY • HAMBURG
STOCKHOLM • ATHENS • TOKYO • MILAN • MADRID
PRAGUE • WARSAW • BUDAPEST • AUCKLAND

To Glen,
with love.

ISBN 0-373-69193-9

MADE IN TEXAS

Copyright © 2004 by Kristine Rolofson.

www.eHarlequin.com

Printed in U.S.A.

"I'm going to kiss you goodnight now," Cal murmured

"Are you sure?" Adelaide smiled at him in the darkness.

"I'm sure," he said, then tugged her closer so their bodies touched. Her full breasts were against his chest and she had the overwhelming desire to rip off his shirt and bury her face in his naked chest. "No more ranch talk. I'm going to take advantage of being in your bedroom for a few minutes."

Oh, good, she wanted to say. Even though she had no business starting something with this cowboy...in her condition. "And how are you going to do that?"

He brushed her cheek with his lips. "I thought I'd kiss you for a while," he whispered. "Maybe a few hours."

"Hours?"

"Mmm." His hand wandered over her hip. "Unlike our first date."

She winced. "Please don't remind me."

"It's one of my fondest memories," he murmured against her mouth. "Up until the end when you ran out of the motel room."

She wasn't running now, she realized. That wide expanse of king-size bed was only inches away, and she couldn't resist spending one night there with Cal.

Well, at least she didn't have to worry about getting pregnant....

Dear Reader,

A magazine article about wealthy women crossed my desk a few months ago. At first I thought my husband was hinting I was spending too much money on eBay again (oh, do I love vintage fabric, much more than mutual funds), but this turned out to be different. The women interviewed explained how having money had changed their lives for better and for worse. One woman, who had inherited a large sum of money from a father she'd barely known, said sadly that she would rather have had the father.

And I, who happen to have had the best father in the universe, cannot imagine what it would have been like to grow up without that special relationship in my life. And so *Made in Texas* was born, centering on a heroine who inherits a fortune but would rather have known the father who amassed it. Money helps renovate her ramshackle Victorian house, but it takes the love of a sexy cowboy to repair Addie's broken family and make her believe in love again.

I hope you enjoy my latest BOOTS & BOOTIES romance! Write to me at P.O. Box 323, Peace Dale, RI 02883.

Happy reading,

Kristine Rolofson

Books by Kristine Rolofson

HARLEQUIN TEMPTATION
877—THE BABY AND THE BACHELOR
906—A MONTANA CHRISTMAS
989—THE BEST MAN IN TEXAS

1

February 14th

ADELAIDE LARSON KNEW she was likely to regret stepping through the doorway of Billy's, a bar with the largest dance floor north of Austin and affectionately known as the "meet market" of central Texas. Next door were two motels, and a diner open till three in the morning, so Billy's was nothing if not convenient for an evening out on the town.

"You know," Addie said to her friend, "I'm not the luckiest person in the world. I could jinx you for the whole night."

"Quit fussing," Kate said, giving her a nudge to walk faster. "And smile, will you? You look like you're going to an execution."

"I'm not ready for this." "This" was a Valentine's party, with no cover charge for the ladies and red roses to be given out at midnight. The amount of red and pink crepe paper streamers hanging from the ceiling was almost obscene, along with the clusters of red and white balloons that filled the corners of the enormous room. Bars lined opposite sides of the building, and a country-western band blasted an old Garth Brooks tune from a stage across the room. The place was filled with people. And smoke. And dancing, drinking, flirting couples.

Addie thought it was like visiting a foreign country.

"You'll feel better once you have a drink," her friend assured her, but Addie wasn't so sure. This kind of thing was easy for Kate, who was different from anyone else Addie knew. Kate had been divorced for almost four years, and thrived on the single life, which is why Addie had decided that her return to the dating world would be chaperoned by an expert.

"I haven't danced since my wedding reception, you know." Which seemed like a century ago, when she was young and pretty and full of dreams. And Jack—no, best not to think about him right now. "I don't think I remember—"

"It's too late to back out now. Your mother's watching the kids and you're free for as long as you want to be. We're going to meet some men and have a good time." She took Addie's arm and hauled her toward the closest bar. "First, a drink. You don't have to dance if you don't want to. We'll see if there's anyone here we know. Give it an hour and if you're really miserable, we'll leave, I promise."

"All right." But she wouldn't leave, Addie thought. Not right away. Part of her wanted to be back home, tucking in her children and watching the latest episode of *The Bachelor* on television, but she was so tired of being alone at night in that sad, little bedroom at the top of the stairs. Getting drunk in a bar on Valentine's Day wasn't exactly the best alternative, but one rum and Coke and a little adult company wouldn't kill her. "I'll do my best."

"Good. Smile. Look like you're having a good time."

"What?" They were closer to the band now and Addie couldn't hear. Kate led her through the crowd clustered around the bar and managed to catch the bartender's eye.

"A beer and—"

"Rum and Coke," Addie shouted. Kate grinned, and three men turned their heads to stare. Men always stared at Kate. She was tall and slender, with long, black hair that waved past her shoulders and halfway to her waist. When she turned her blue eyes on men of any age, they did everything but drop to their knees and kiss her snakeskin boots. Addie, on the other hand, was not the least bit statuesque, with nothing about her to make men stop and stare with their mouths hanging open. The only guys who lit up when she walked through the door were five years old and dependent on her for food.

Which is why she'd let Kate fix her makeup and redo her chin-length hair into something spiky and, as Kate said, "totally hot." Which meant her light brown hair now had gold highlights and gelled tips. She'd borrowed one of Kate's ice-white Lycra T-shirts, with a modest rounded neck, but refused to wiggle into a pair of jeans that hung below her belly button. As she'd told Kate, a woman who'd once given birth to twins had no business strutting around with her stomach exposed.

"You look good," Kate said into her ear after she handed Addie her drink. "But you're still wincing, like you'd rather be helping out at the kindergarten than dancing the two-step with some good-looking guy."

"I would."

"Pretend." Kate laughed, prompting several jean-clad men to step closer and start a conversation. Addie sipped from the plastic cup and tried to remember what it was like when she was young, single and sure that life was going to turn out exactly the way she wanted it to. But that was a long time ago, and she was tired of thinking about it and, inevitably, feeling sorry for herself.

Which was not at all attractive.

And even boring.

"Wanna dance?"

She looked up from her drink to see a pleasant-looking young man holding out his hand to her. "Uh—"

"Go." Kate plucked the cup from her hand and set it on the bar. "Have fun."

"Well—" She hesitated, but no one seemed to notice. She was lonely. So lonely that the pain of it threatened to eat her from the inside out. She wondered if anyone could see it, that loneliness seeping out of her skin and turning her gray and cold. She wondered if there was anyone else in this giant room who understood what it was like to live with that unending feeling of loss.

"Cool." The kid—she couldn't help wondering if he was old enough to drink—took her hand and hauled her out to the dance floor. Addie attempted a smile and told herself it was time she got on with her life.

At Billy's and everywhere else.

CAL HAD BEEN DAMN GLAD to get to town, even though he'd gotten in later than he'd planned. He needed a few cold beers to wash the dust down tonight. It had been one hell of a week, but he was free now, and tomorrow was Sunday, meaning an easy day with few chores and an afternoon to do whatever he damn well pleased. It wasn't until he noticed the number of cars packed into the parking lot, and beyond, in a nearby field, that he remembered it was Valentine's Day.

Which, if he remembered correctly, was an easy day to get laid if you were a young guy with any kind of brains. But he wasn't young and he wasn't feeling particularly intelligent, either. Not that he wouldn't react if a pretty, young thing winked at him, but those days were pretty much long gone. He'd gotten used to things the way they were, meaning he was fast closing in on forty and he sure as hell was no prize. The women had stopped flirting years ago, and so had he.

But Cal *was* thirsty. And Billy's always had pretty good music and a crowd worth watching. A man could lean on the bar and get an eyeful of good-looking ladies in skimpy tops and tight jeans while he drank a beer or two and remembered what it was like to be young and crazy.

He wasn't disappointed either, once he'd handed over the cover charge and made his way through those pink streamers hanging from the ceiling. He kicked a few balloons out of his way as he walked to the closest corner of the bar. The noise was almost deafening and the place was packed wall-to-wall with people having a good time.

Cal ordered a beer and watched a tall, black-haired beauty hold court at a nearby table, one of the few that lined the wall farthest from the band. She chose to dance with a heavyset man who looked like he wrestled steers for a living. They disappeared onto the dance floor, leaving a blond woman at the table with a handful of guys who didn't look pleased to be left behind. Cal watched the blonde refuse to dance with any of them, which meant she was either married or ticked off about something. She looked young—not yet thirty, he guessed. Not that he could see her face very well, but he figured she must be pretty decent-looking or she'd be sitting by herself.

Cal shifted, his attention distracted by the arrival of his beer and a question from a redhead who wanted him to pass her the ashtray by his elbow. By the time he thought about the blonde again, she was long gone from that back table. He supposed she'd given up and danced with someone after all, so Cal eyed the band, drank another beer and relaxed. He didn't have anything to complain about: he was off the ranch and had money in his wallet and gas in his truck, which was paid for as of two weeks ago.

He stayed for over an hour, long enough to quench his thirst and feel human again. He'd talked to some old friends he hadn't seen for months, discussed the weather with a couple of ranchers' sons who were up to no good and laughed with one of the bartenders over the commotion a Shania Twain look-alike was causing due to her low-cut jeans and halter top. It was after midnight when Cal decided he'd had enough. Oh, a few years back he'd have asked two or three women to dance—he did a respectable two-step and a damn fine waltz—but now he'd been content to watch from the sidelines. The bar had become uncomfortably crowded and he'd grown tired of being elbowed and jostled.

"I'm so sorry." A soft voice interrupted his thoughts about leaving, especially when he looked down into a pair of blue eyes swimming in unshed tears.

"About what?" For the life of him, he couldn't understand why the woman looked upset. She was pretty—despite the weird brownish-blond hair and too much eye makeup—with flawless, pale skin, and lips that could tempt a man to forget his age. She was in her twenties, he guessed. Too young for an old cowboy, he reminded himself. But there was something familiar about her, a face he'd seen before somewhere.

Her gaze dropped to his boots, and he looked down to see them covered in liquid. "I just spilled my drink on your boots," she said. Yeah, she had. And the world was going to keep on spinning. "I didn't mean to, of course, but somebody hit my arm."

"Is that why you're crying?"

Her chin lifted, a stubborn chin in a heart-shaped face. "I'm not crying."

"My mistake."

She set her empty cup on the bar. "Your boots—"

"Have survived worse," he interjected. They were new, his Christmas present to himself, but he figured they'd clean up okay. "Can I buy you another?"

"Another drink?"

"Yeah."

"Oh, no. Thanks." There was the briefest smile before she looked sad again. "I think I'm going to go home now." She looked toward the table where the black-haired woman he'd noticed earlier stood cozying up to a guy large enough to have played linebacker for UT. She was the blond he'd noticed before, the one refusing to dance with her friend's admirers.

"What about your friend?" He gestured toward the tall, laughing woman.

"She said she had a ride home." Again, there was that brief smile, then a flash of pain in her eyes when she glanced up at him.

"You don't come here very often, do you." He didn't ask it as a question. The woman clearly looked over her head in a bar loaded with singles trying to hook up and couples whose intentions for later on were obvious.

"This is my first time at Billy's. And probably my last," she admitted, sounding as disappointed as if she'd just flunked out of school. He wanted to chuckle, but he thought he'd hurt her feelings if he did. She looked so damn depressed about being here, and a few moments ago he'd thought she was going to start crying.

"So," he said, feeling ridiculously protective and more than a little intrigued, "your friend dragged you here to have a good time."

"Yes. But it didn't quite work out that way."

"Why not?" He set his empty beer bottle on the counter of the bar and leaned closer so he could hear her words better. "You were hoping to meet someone, right?" He took her hand in his as the band started a country rendition of "The Tennessee Waltz." There was no law that said he couldn't change his mind and ask a lady to dance.

"No," she said, looking down at his hand clasping hers.

"No, you won't dance with me? Or no, you weren't hoping to meet somebody?" He didn't wait for an answer. Instead he kept her hand in his and eased through the crowd, making room for both of them to move away from the bar and get closer to the dance floor. A lot of other couples had the same idea, because the area was filling up fast.

"Neither, I guess."

"Good answer. Where are you from?"

"Austin," she said, looking up at him. "And you?"

"Nowhere." She tilted her head as if she thought he was joking, so he smiled. "Really. You've never heard of Nowhere?"

"A man from nowhere," she murmured. "Perfect. I've always liked this song," she said, as he took her in his arms. She placed her hand on his shoulder and looked up at him. "I guess one dance won't hurt."

Looking back, Cal wasn't sure how it happened. Oh, they danced a few more slow tunes together—the band was loading up the set with love songs in honor of Valentine's Day—and they talked easily about books and movies and music when the band took a break between sets. And when the music started again, Cal held her closer and she rested her cheek against his chest. He decided he liked the feel of that warm, little body against his, and maybe she wasn't too young for him after all. It had been years since he'd met a woman he might want to know better.

And he didn't even know her name.

So when she said she had to leave, he offered to walk her to her car like any true gentleman would. He would ask for her name and phone number.

"I have pepper spray on my key chain," she told him, hesitating at the door to grab a hooded jacket from a heaping coatrack. It was raining again. "I'll be fine."

"It's still not a good idea for a lady to walk alone in parking lots after midnight," Cal said. Maybe she'd want to have dinner sometime. Or maybe he was being foolish even thinking about dating anyone.

And when she unlocked her car door and turned to thank him, he felt ten feet tall. He'd enjoyed himself, he told her.

"Thanks for being so nice about your boots. And thanks for the company." She surprised him by reaching up and kissing his cheek. He'd turned his head to say good-night at the same time, so his lips brushed hers. But it didn't stop at a mere touching of lips, because he leaned closer and kissed her again, this time with a deliberate meeting of mouths that threatened to drop them both to the dirt. Her arms reached, clung to his neck, while he held her warm body against his and kissed her with an unexpected need of his own.

Their tongues met and mated. His hands swept her back and tugged her shirt from the waistband of her jeans so he could slide his hands along the warm, bare skin of her back. She didn't stop him, simply moved closer, as if being touched by him was exactly what she wanted, right now, right here.

"Get a room," someone called, followed by male and female laughter.

He was crazy, caressing a strange woman in a parking lot behind a bar. He lifted his head, but only a fraction of an inch.

"I have to go," she whispered against his mouth, but she didn't pull away. Despite the cold rain that wet their heads and ran down their faces, he kept holding her in the darkness. Her mouth was warm against his, and his hands swept low, cupping her bottom.

"Don't go," he said, pulling her tight against him. Cal knew need when he tasted it. "Not yet."

"Okay."

He didn't know how long they kissed out there in the darkness, but he knew it was never going to be enough. By the time he paused to catch his breath, he could feel the rain dripping past his collar, onto his neck. It was like being crazy, with no thoughts in his head except how good she felt and how sweet she tasted. "You want to stop?"

"Not yet," she said, echoing his earlier words.

Her small hands were inside his shirt, and he would have tossed it to the ground if they'd been anywhere but the parking lot at Billy's. She gasped when he lifted her into his arms.

"What are you doing?"

"Getting out of the rain." He strode past the rows of cars, toward the neon Vacancy sign in the window of the Sleepy Time Motel, the newer one of the two facing the main road. "Getting some privacy."

He listened for her protest, but she wrapped her arms around his neck and rested her head on his shoulder as if he had been carrying her to bed for years. He didn't know if she'd stay or not. He didn't know what was going to happen in the next few hours. But kissing her was like coming alive again after a long, cold winter. And he thought she might feel the same way.

So, what the hell.

He carried her right into the empty lobby, a small room with a counter and a couple of vinyl chairs. He was afraid if he let her go, she'd disappear, so he rang the bell and waited for someone to show up from the back room. Getting his wallet out of his back pocket took some doing, but within a couple of minutes, the yawning old man had given him a key and a room number.

"You've done this before," she said, looking up at him with an uncertain expression.

"A few times, for friends who were too drunk to drive home." Cal pushed the door open with his foot and stepped out into the rain once again. "Believe it or not," he said, holding her closer against him to shield her from the weather, "this is the first time with, uh, female company."

"Female company," she repeated, then smiled. "That sounds so old-fashioned."

"I'm an old-fashioned guy." He found the right door and was forced to set the woman on her feet so he could unlock it. Once the door swung open, they hurried inside to the stuffy interior. Cal shut the door behind them and didn't turn on the lights; the glow from the streetlight through the picture window was enough to outline the furniture. The bed—its wide mattress looking as big as Texas—was easily visible.

"I've never done anything like this before, either," she whispered. He took her cold hands in his and tried to warm them with his own. "Kiss me," she said. "So I don't think about changing my mind."

"I will kiss you for as long as you like." Cal brushed his mouth against hers. Her lips were cold and her cheeks were wet. "All night, even."

"I don't have all night." She pulled her hands away from his and reached for his shirt, which was still unbuttoned. Her touch threatened his self-control, but he did his best to keep from lifting her onto the bed and tumbling down on the mattress on top of her. He kissed her mouth, her jaw, her ear, while her fingers smoothed his chest and drove him to the edge of sanity. He backed up to the bed and sat down, the blue-eyed woman standing between his open knees. She shrugged off her damp jacket and tossed it aside, leaving Cal free to lift her T-shirt. She quickly pulled it over her head and dropped it to the floor.

"You're not married, are you?" He set his mouth over one lace-covered breast, and she held her breath, as if afraid to move and stop him. His hands framed her waist, but he felt her sigh and tremble.

She hesitated for the briefest of moments. "No. You?"

"No." And he had never been happier about that in his entire life. She smelled like roses and vanilla, looked like a goddess and—for now—she was all his.

"Have you ever been?" It took a moment for the question to register, since he'd grown harder with every second he'd kissed her. Cal reached behind her and unhooked the bra's catch, then eased the straps down her arms.

"No," Cal managed to reply, despite the tempting vision of a half-naked woman standing in front of him. Her breasts were beautiful, soft and round, and thankfully she made no move to cover them. "Never."

His heart in his throat, Cal watched her unsnap her jeans and kick off her boots before she stepped closer to him. He stood, removing his own boots and clothing in record time, and reached for her, a lovely silhouette in the dim light of the room.

Skin to skin, mouth to mouth, Calvin George Ennis McDonald figured he'd died and gone to heaven. The woman in his arms was passionate and warm, soft and demanding, all satin skin and hot need. Somehow they managed to toss the bed-covers aside and land together on the bed, neither noticing the cold temperature of the sheets. And somehow Cal managed to remember the condom he kept in his wallet—a habit left over from a wild youth—and when he would have slowed down, she urged him closer. And then he was between her legs, and with one smooth motion he was inside of all that tight, female warmth.

Her eyes were closed, but she grasped his shoulders and lifted her hips to meet his thrusts. She urged him deeper, and Cal, too long without a woman, didn't even try to slow down. She climaxed quickly, her hands pressed tight on his arms. Cal gave in to the pure pleasure of her body and, with a few quick thrusts, found his own release.

He'd shocked himself. Not with his need, for it had been a long time since he'd made love to a woman, but because he didn't have sex with strangers. And here in the bed was a woman whose name he didn't know, who still had her eyes closed when he rolled off her and onto his back.

Her arm went over her eyes, as if to shield them from a light that didn't exist. Cal didn't know what to say, so he lay quiet and waited for the pounding of his heart to ease before turning to look at the woman he'd just made love to. If you could call that "making love." It had been more like raw need at its most powerful. "Are you okay?"

"I'm fine," she whispered, though her voice sounded choked. She was crying, he realized. He noticed that tears were snaking along the side of her face, though he still couldn't see her eyes. He knew better than to turn a light on, but he sure as hell didn't know what to do with a weeping woman in his bed.

"I'm sorry," he tried, hoping that would make things better.

"It's not your fault." She lowered her arm and wiped her face on a corner of the sheet before modestly covering herself with the rest of it. "Could you turn away, please, so I can get dressed?"

"All right." Cal moved over to the other side of

the bed and swung his legs over the edge of the mattress. He wondered what she was crying about, and what wasn't his fault, but it didn't seem like the time to ask. He would give her time to dress and then he would turn around and try to talk to her. But right now he was naked as a jay-bird and still half aroused, the condom thankfully in place, and he'd look downright ridiculous strutting around the motel room picking up his clothes.

"I'm done," she said. "The room's all yours."

He turned to see her looking flushed, her blond hair still spiky and appealingly messy. She looked terribly young all of a sudden and he wanted nothing more than to take her in his arms and tell her it was okay.

"Give me a minute," he said instead. "I'll walk you—"

"No." She was out the door in a flash. Cal hurried to get dressed, but that turned out to take more time than he'd figured. By the time he raced across the parking lot, she was already in her car.

"Your name," he called. "What is it?"

The woman shook her head and rolled up the window, shutting her away from him. She turned away and put the car in gear. In a heartbeat she was gone, the small car's taillights disappearing into the night.

Cal walked to his truck and climbed inside. He

was so damn tired, he thought about spending the rest of the night in the motel room, but decided against it. There was no point torturing himself with the scent of a woman on the pillows and the odd realization that she didn't want to know his name.

He'd go back where he belonged.

ADDIE HAD DONE SOME STUPID things in her life, but last night topped the list. Cursing quietly in a hot shower had done little to ease her embarrassment—or the realization that she'd behaved like a lonely, love-starved woman who couldn't resist the appeal of a few kisses and had ended up on her back in a motel room. No, nothing she'd done since arriving home last night had made her feel better about what had happened.

Blaming her behavior on too much rum would have been an easy way to excuse herself. But Lord knows those rum and Cokes hadn't helped.

The whole thing had been so out of character that Addie knew no one would believe her. If she cared to confess to one of her friends, that is. Which she didn't. This secret would go to her grave, and if she was very, very lucky—which she wasn't—she would never see that man again. And even if she did, she would pretend not to recognize the good-looking cowboy who had danced with her. And kissed her. And carried her across a parking lot to a motel.

Addie made herself a pot of very strong coffee and prayed the boys would sleep later than six. Her mother, last night's babysitter, was thankfully still asleep in the spare bedroom, and hadn't seen her daughter arrive home with her clothes rumpled and her underwear stuffed in her jacket pocket.

2

April 1st

"MRS. LARSON?" THE LAWYER coughed politely and waited for Adelaide to lift her head off his glass-topped desk, but she was in no hurry. Especially since the room was spinning around her and she had to concentrate on staying in the chair. Falling on the floor in a dead faint was not at all the image she wanted to project while in a meeting with her deceased father's lawyer. She'd dressed in her best black pants and her favorite taupe knit top, the one she thought made her look sophisticated when she wore it with taupe dangle earrings and bronze lip shimmer. She'd wanted to look her best, and here she was making a spectacle of herself. Some things never changed.

"Adelaide, are you all right?" She heard the scrape of the chair as her mother drew closer and began to pat her between the shoulder blades.

"Leave it to Eddie to cause problems even after he's dead and buried."

"Mom," Addie muttered, willing her to stop talking. She loved her mother—Paula Johanson had raised her single-handedly and with a devotion that stopped just short of obsession—but Paula had never forgiven her ex-husband for his many sins, one of which was walking out on his family. And she wasn't shy about discussing those sins, either. "Please don't say anything. Not now."

"You should put your head between your legs," her mother said.

"I can't...breathe," Addie managed to say after doing what she was told.

"Here," Mr. Anders said, sliding a paper bag across the desk as Addie lifted her head. "We find that breathing into a bag helps."

"Good idea." Her mother nodded her approval.

She tried it, wondering how many times a week the plump, balding lawyer faced fainting clients. Probably more times than she'd imagine. After long moments of breathing, while her mother discussed financial options with Mr. Anders, Addie felt well enough to put the bag down.

"She fainted when the doctor told her she was expecting twins, too," Paula informed the lawyer. "Adelaide's a little sensitive to surprises."

"Well, that's certainly, uh, unfortunate," he

mumbled, tapping the stack of papers in front of him. "Are you feeling well enough to continue, Mrs. Larson? We can reschedule, if you like, but we're almost at the end now."

"Yes," Addie said, but she kept the paper bag in her lap and tried not to fidget with it while the lawyer droned on about stocks and bonds, trust funds, inheritance taxes and properties. She didn't remember much about her father, and her memories mostly came from old photographs of the three of them together when she was still in diapers, toddling across the front lawn of the house on Oakdale Drive. In one, he had short, blond hair and wore a psychedelic orange T-shirt over blue jeans. He had smiled at the camera, but the expression looked forced, as if he was making an effort to enjoy family life. Her mother had stood slightly apart from him, and her smile, as always, had been for her daughter.

"And you'll be able to take possession immediately," Mr. Anders concluded with a relieved air. He placed a small, manila envelope in front of her. "All the keys are inside. I'm sure you'll want to inspect the property, but I will warn you that the house itself is quite old. It's the land around it that's valuable. I've included the appraisal of the property with the papers, and you already have an offer—"

"Someone wants to buy it?" Addie's mother didn't try to hide her excitement. "Oh, Adelaide, this is so wonderful!"

"Mom," Addie cautioned, "let Mr. Anders finish."

"Sorry." She patted her daughter's back. "How are you feeling? Do you need to take a little break from this, get some coffee, some air, maybe a little something to eat?"

"I'm okay." She wasn't okay. Not at all. She was numb and dizzy and wanted to cry, but she wasn't about to shed tears in front of anyone. Not over a father she'd hardly known, that was certain. And not because she'd just discovered that she was wealthy beyond her wildest dreams. *I've had enough surprises this winter,* she wanted to shout, but she gripped her hands together in her lap and crushed the edge of the paper bag instead.

"You look a little pale," Paula fumed, but Addie ignored her and met Mr. Anders's gaze.

"Please," she said, "let's continue. You said there was an offer?"

"For the two commercial building lots in San Marcos, yes. But your father hoped you would keep the ranch itself in the family," the lawyer reminded her. "I believe I explained that a few minutes ago? I think your father hoped you would live there, but—"

"As if he has any business giving orders to a daughter he never saw," Paula muttered.

"But," Mr. Anders continued, "if you decide to sell, there are some conditions that will have to be met, according to the codicil on page forty-one."

"I understand," Addie told the lawyer, although she wasn't sure she did. Not exactly. But she knew one thing—that she would now be able to take her children to live in her very own house where no rent was due. She could quit her job, thank goodness. And buy the boys new clothes, and go out to dinner without guilt. This must be what winning the lottery felt like, if only she could feel well enough to enjoy it.

"If you'll just sign one more document," Mr. Anders said, showing her the last paper, with a red X next to a signature line. "Then we're done. If I can be of any further help to you, please contact the office at any time. I realize this has been overwhelming."

"Thank you." She signed her name, Adelaide L. Larson, in neat script. She ignored another wave of dizziness, and prayed that she could exit the lawyer's oak and leather office without being sick all over the expensive Oriental carpet.

"Now, do you know where your father's land is located?" He opened another folder and pulled out a photocopied map of central Texas.

"Not really."

"Approximately seventy miles north of Austin." He drew a circle around a town before handing her the map. "There."

"In Nowhere?" The dizziness swung through her head again as she saw the name of the town.

Her mother peered over her shoulder. "Leave it to Eddie to live in a town called that." She laughed, and even the lawyer smiled.

"It's supposed to be quite picturesque. Have you ever been there?" he asked Addie.

"No, but I've heard of it," she admitted and was glad she was too old to blush. She'd made a foolish, stupid, careless mistake six weeks ago. With a man from Nowhere. He'd made a joke of it; he'd made her laugh. It had been quite flattering, until she'd come to her senses and raced out of the motel room. Not one of her shining moments as a responsible human being and sensible mother of two, and one she wasn't likely to forget.

Paula frowned. "It's not a place I remember him talking about. I wonder why he stayed in Texas. I figured he'd headed for California or Mexico."

Addie felt it important that Mr. Anders understand. "We thought he'd died years ago. He didn't keep in touch."

"Not a paternal bone in the man's body," Paula said. "Not your fault, honey, but at least he came through for you once in his life, when he made out his will. Too bad you have to move, but maybe it's for the best. And a year goes by fast, though I can't imagine what the house must look like. Your father never cared much what people thought." She faced the lawyer. "What's this ranch like?"

"I've never been there. I didn't know your, uh, ex-husband very well," the man admitted. "He came in one day and asked for help drawing up his will. I'd had a cancellation and, well, we took care of business. Mr. Johanson wasn't much for small talk. We mailed papers back and forth, but we never met again. I suspect he had a little of the hermit in him."

"More than a little," Paula pointed out. "He never did have much to say. Not even 'good-bye.'"

Addie thanked Mr. Anders again. They discussed the weather—unseasonably rainy for the first of April—while his secretary made copies of the signed documents. She looked at her watch and realized she was late picking up the boys from Kate's. She crammed the proof of her inheritance into her tote bag and hurried her mother out of the lawyer's office before Paula could make any more remarks about the deceased man who'd left his daughter hundreds of thousands of dollars, a ranch and an unfortunate reason to move to Nowhere.

"Come on, Mom," she said, searching through her bag for her car keys. "I need to get the boys."

"We can't go out to lunch first?" Paula pushed the heavy glass door open and hesitated before stepping out into the rain. "It's almost noon. I could use a cup of coffee, and you look like you haven't eaten in a week. Are you sure you're feeling okay?"

No, she wanted to say. *I have never been worse*. But instead the words "I'm fine" came out of her mouth once again. She followed her mother outside, but Paula didn't budge from the protection of the roof's overhang.

"We're going to get something to eat," her mother ordered in her best don't-bother-to-argue voice, at the same time pointing to a restaurant across the street. "You can call Kate and tell her that we'll be home in an hour and a half. I'll treat the new heiress to a hamburger and a chocolate shake."

Addie's stomach protested at the thought of grease and milk. "What I'd really like is a bowl of soup."

"Then soup it is. We'll celebrate properly tonight," her mother continued. "How about I get us a couple of steaks and a bottle of champagne? We'll toast Eddie, who came through at the end, even if he wasn't worth much when he was alive."

"No champagne," she managed to say. "No celebration."

"Oh, dear, honey," her mother crooned, putting an arm around Addie's shoulders. "You're feeling bad about your father and I'm acting like a bitter, middle-aged woman when I actually got over the man years ago and moved on with my life. And now he's gone and you never knew him, which might have been a good thing, may he rest in peace, but Addie, honey, you've got to look on the bright side."

"The bright side?" Addie repeated, taking deep breaths of fresh air through her nose and breathing slowly out through her mouth, the way she'd heard reduced stress. She had the flu, she told herself for possibly the two hundredth time. This wasn't morning sickness. *He had used a condom.* "I know what the bright side is, Mom."

"An inheritance. Financial freedom. A fresh start. A bright future for you and your family."

"You sound like an infomercial."

Paula laughed and took her daughter's elbow. "Becoming rich hasn't spoiled your sense of humor. Come on," she said, urging her into the rain. "Soup it is."

"Wait," Addie said, knowing once and for all there was going to be no fighting this. She thrust the tote bag full of papers into her mother's arms and threw up in Mr. Anders's marble urn.

Which of course made perfect sense, according

to the Adelaide Larson Rules of Life: every silver
cloud had a black lining, complete with lightning,
hail and torrential rains.

"HELL AND DAMNATION, this weather's getting to
me."

"You're griping about a little rain again?" Cal
grinned. John had complained about the weather
for as long as Cal had known him, which was
going on fifteen years now.

"Well, I'm close to eighty, you know," the old
man blustered. He stared out the open barn door
and watched the rain soak the yard. "I've had
enough rain to last me a lifetime. This arthur-itis
is going to be the death of me, 'specially my
damned legs."

"You'd better move to Arizona, then." Cal
tipped his hat back and eyed the gray sky. "Get
yourself into one of those senior citizens' places
and learn how to play bingo with the ladies."

"Yeah, well, you think you're funny, but you
never know what could happen to either one of us
now that Ed's gone." John wore an ancient ball cap
with John Deere scrawled across the top in thick,
green letters that had faded to an odd shade of yellow. He liked to say the cap and the tractor were the
only things his wife left him with when she'd run
off fifty or so years ago. "I'm too old to start over."

"You've got a lifetime lease on your place," Cal reminded him. But they both knew that whoever took over the Triple J could do exactly as he damned well pleased. Leases could be broken, land could be sold, and there wasn't a darn thing Cal and John could do about it except bitch a little and then move on.

But neither one of them wanted to. Cal faced a busy calving season and John was the best horse trainer in the county. Ed had been at a stock sale when he'd dropped dead of a heart attack after bidding on a fine herd of mares destined for greatness—or at least the start of a quarter horse breeding program. John had taken the whole thing pretty hard, not coming out of his small home east of the bunkhouse for three days after the cremation.

Now they had eight new mares and no boss.

At least, no boss they'd met yet. Oh, a lawyer and some bank people had roamed around the place and taken a lot of notes, asked a few questions and driven back to Austin in their fancy SUVs, but there'd been no word from anyone since.

"He had a kid," John said, easing his bulk onto a bale of hay. He stretched out his legs and winced. "Did I ever tell you that?"

"No, but I saw a picture in his room one time." About four years ago he'd caught his boss holding a picture—the kind with a black plastic frame and cardboard on the back. Ed had been staring at that photo as if he was trying to fit himself inside the thing. Cal caught a glimpse of a pretty girl in a graduation cap before Ed put the picture back in his dresser drawer.

"Yeah?"

"A girl."

"I dunno," John sighed. "He never said much about it."

Cal could understand that. There were some things better kept quiet, like picking up a strangely vulnerable woman in a bar, ending up in a motel and then—disaster. He still winced whenever he remembered that night. She'd been sweet and wild and he'd been hot and stupid. Of course it had ended up in a mess, convincing Cal that he had been right to avoid the complications that came with women. Like flies on horses, problems buzzing everywhere.

"No wonder monks look so damn peaceful."

"Huh?" John stared at him. "Monks? You don't know any monks. What the hell are you talkin' about, son?"

"Just thinking out loud," he explained. "There was a show about monks on the History Channel last night."

"Not natural," the old man grumbled. "All those men living together and not talking."

"Without women," Cal added, unwillingly remembering the oddest Valentine's Day he'd ever experienced.

"I'll bet they don't have TV, either." John hauled himself off the hay bale and headed for the barn door. "It's just not natural."

"Yeah." Cal couldn't help chuckling at the old man's disgust. "No football, basketball, baseball—"

"No ESPN," John muttered. "Them monks don't know what they're missing. I'm heading home. Got a stew in the Crock-Pot that's enough for both of us, if you want."

"Thanks, but I'm all set. I've got cows to check on before I call it a night."

"You need help?"

He shook his head. "Go on. I feel like a drive, that's all."

The old man hesitated before stepping into the rainy darkness. "You can get a job anywhere, Cal. Good men like you are hard to find."

"I'm not worried." But he was. After twenty years, the Triple J had become home. Cal wasn't looking forward to starting over.

AFTER READING THROUGH most of the paperwork given to her by her father's lawyer, Addie came to realize that just because she had inherited a great deal of property didn't mean that her financial problems were over. Oh, there was some money in her father's bank accounts, but she'd have to wait until some of the land was sold before she had extra cash.

"Sell it all," her mother said, eyeing the array of legal papers spread across the kitchen table. "Buy yourself a nice three-bedroom town house. Round Rock has good schools, you know. Make yourself a home, honey. Lord knows you deserve some good fortune. Make the most of it."

"I can't just put everything up for sale, not without looking at it first."

"Sure you can." Paula popped open a can of diet cola and leaned against the kitchen counter. "Call a real estate agent and give her the list of properties and the current evaluations. Let someone else take care of this."

"I want to see the ranch."

"Why?"

"It's where my father lived." She shrugged. "I guess I'm curious."

Her mother sighed. "I suppose I'd be curious, too, if I were in your shoes. What Eddie's done, and where he was all these years, has sure been a mystery. And to think he was only seventy or so miles away. I could have passed him on the streets of Austin and never known it."

"So you'll go?"

"Go?" Paula frowned, creasing an otherwise unlined forehead. She looked younger than her fifty-three years. Her gray-streaked blond hair was cut to chin length, her skin held few wrinkles and her blue eyes usually shone with good humor. She could talk a blue streak, but Addie knew that her mother's common sense had successfully gotten her through a life that hadn't been easy.

"Go with us to see the Triple J. That's its name."

"When? I can't take any more days off right now."

"Saturday, then. We'll take the boys and make an adventure out of it. I've been doing a lot of thinking this afternoon," Addie said, motioning for her mother to sit down. The boys, watching *Sesame Street* in the living room, were finally content to sit still for ten minutes. And Addie, now that her stomach had settled down, had convinced herself once again that she simply had a touch of the flu.

"It's a wonder you can concentrate, being sick and all," her mother said, clearing a place at the small table.

"I'm feeling fine now, Mom. Look—" Addie pointed to the list of assets "—this should belong to you. All of it. It's not fair that my father left everything to me."

"Of course it is." Paula's eyes filled with tears.

"It's more fair than anything I can think of. Who deserves the money more?"

"You do. I say we split this, fifty-fifty."

"No. I have my job and my condo, and I'm fine. I don't need anything from Eddie Johanson at this stage of my life. What matters is that you and the boys have a secure future now."

"I would rather have had a father." She sighed, remembering how thrilled Jack had been when she'd told him she was pregnant. "And now my boys don't have one, either."

"You'll marry again," her mother assured her. "You're still young. You'll meet someone."

"Someone who wants to be a father to someone else's kids?" Addie thought of the tall man at Billy's. He'd had kind eyes and the kind of face that a woman liked looking at, not too handsome and not too cute. His body had been lean and strongly muscled, and his large hands knew how to touch a woman. He'd used a condom. *He'd used a condom.* There was no reason to think there was anything wrong with her that chicken soup and saltine crackers couldn't fix.

3

"Next stop, Nowhere!" Addie turned to make sure that the boys hadn't wriggled out of their seat belts or car seats. Her sons were stocky versions of their father, with light brown hair and eyes. They grinned at her, though Ian's smile was wider than Matt's. Younger by two minutes, Matthew was the one who liked to think things over and take his time deciding on things. Rambunctious Ian usually led the way, but if his twin decided on an opposite game or venture, he invariably gave in. Matthew was nothing if not stubborn.

Like his father, whose last words to his wife, on his cell phone, had been, "Don't worry. I'm fine." And he'd fallen asleep at the wheel and crashed into a tree. So much for being careful. And so much for promises.

"You look terrible," Paula grumbled, adjusting her sunglasses. "You're not sleeping well, again, are you?"

"No," Addie confessed. "There's a lot to think

about." Like what the ranch would look like, and if she would want to live there. And should she buy a pregnancy test. She'd lain awake for the past two nights wondering what would happen next. At least she didn't have to worry about having enough money. Yet she worried about making stupid mistakes with what she'd inherited.

"I know you've got a lot on your mind, honey, but take it one thing at a time. That's what you've done since Jack died, and you've done real well."

"Thanks." But she didn't think that "one day at a time" stuff worked for everything. It didn't help insomnia, and it wasn't going to help with a pile of legal papers and the death of a father she'd never known. And it wasn't going to make any magic if she was unmarried and pregnant and didn't know the father's name—and didn't want to. What was she supposed to tell her family? Her mother was going to have a stroke. And her kids weren't old enough to ask questions now, but someday they'd want to know where their little brother or sister had come from.

Why, from Billy's bar, on Highway 35, she'd say. A lot of Texas babies come from there.

"First you look at this ranch, get it out of your system. And then you put those building lots—where are they?"

"San Marcos."

"Fine. San Marcos. I told you two nights ago, you put those up for sale and then you buy yourself a nice, new car."

"We're *both* buying new cars, Mom."

"I don't want Eddie's money, Adelaide."

"You're going to refuse a gift from your daughter?" She grinned at her mother, who didn't return the smile.

"Yes, I most certainly am." She unfolded a Texas map that was on the seat. "How far away is this place?"

"A little over seventy miles."

"Good heavens. If you actually decide to move there, that'll put an end to my babysitting."

"No, it won't, because you're moving with me."

"You're full of nonsense."

"You've said a thousand times that you're tired of Austin and the traffic. And you can't wait until you retire from teaching. You've said that a thousand times, too."

"Well," Paula grumbled, "that doesn't mean I want to spend the rest of my life taking care of cows."

"Who said anything about cows?"

"It's a ranch, sweetheart. Cows are what make ranches, well, ranches."

"Neither one of us knows anything about ranching, Mom. But it might be a great place to raise the boys, as long as it's not too far from a town."

"Well, don't get your hopes up." Paula tossed the map aside and frowned at the traffic. "If Eddie had money to buy property and stocks, he sure wasn't putting money into keeping a nice house. He pinched every penny he had, right down to our honeymoon. My folks gave us a real nice party in the church basement, cake and punch and little sandwiches, and then off we went, in Eddie's old Buick. It broke down before we got to San Antonio, so we spent the next two days in a motel next to an auto body shop so Ed could do the work on the car himself."

"You never told me that before."

"To this day, I can't stand the smell of car grease." She made a face. "Reminds me of my honeymoon."

Addie couldn't help laughing, which she suspected was exactly what her mother had in mind. "Did you ever get to San Antonio?"

"No. But I did get pregnant."

"I guess being a father scared him?"

"Truly?" Paula shrugged. "I don't know. I guess I never really understood him. We were as different as night and day. So one day, when you were about two, we had another argument and he walked out. I thought he'd gone to cool off somewhere, you know, get a beer and calm down, the way he always did. But I never saw him again."

"Not even for the divorce?"

"Not even then. No one knew where the man went off to. If I'd known he was still in Texas, I would have hunted him down and made him explain himself. But then again, he wasn't much for explaining things. I thought he was the strong, silent type, and then the 'silent' part was what was so hard on the marriage. That man wasn't much of a talker."

"I wonder how he died. Did the lawyer say?"

"No." Paula sighed. "I guess I should have thought to ask."

"I think we were in shock that morning."

"Well, sweetie, I'm sure we'll get all the answers you want when we get to Nowhere." She shook her head. "What a name!"

But Nowhere, to their surprise, turned out to be a pleasant-looking town. Antique stores lined the main street, along with one large restaurant, two coffee shops and an array of quaint storefronts that housed lawyers, a shoe store, bank, post office and bakery. A large town hall stood on one corner, surrounded by green lawn and sidewalks, and at the edge of town was a Dairy Queen.

"So far so good," Addie said, realizing that she hadn't seen a tall, muscular, rancher-type man with dark hair walking down the sidewalk. Maybe she really would never see him again. Or maybe he didn't live in Nowhere at all. And if she was very lucky—which she wasn't, of course—he would have moved to Alaska. Her mother thought she was commenting on the looks of the town.

"I see school signs, but no school." Paula turned to reassure her grandsons that she would buy them ice cream later on, but only if they were very good. "How much farther is this ranch of yours?"

"Only six or seven miles."

"You think real long and hard before deciding to move way out here," her mother said. "Don't make any hasty decisions."

"I won't," Addie promised. The last hasty decision she'd made resulted in morning sickness. One of these days she was going to have to buy a pregnancy test kit and find out, once and for all, what was going on with her body. But Addie knew that as soon as she did that, she could be faced with something she wasn't ready to explain. She let the thought of having a little girl in pink ruffles float through her brain, and reached into her purse for another saltine cracker.

OF COURSE ADDIE FELL in love with the house. Paula watched her daughter's face light up when she stepped out of the car and saw the old, three-story, gabled monstrosity. It needed paint. It probably needed a new roof. And if the outside was any indication of the inside, it was going to need an army of carpenters and repairmen.

But Paula saw her daughter's expression and kept quiet. She hadn't seen such a look of happiness in years. And Addie, who loved nothing more than painting and papering and decorating, who watched the design shows on HGTV, who had owned not one but three doll houses when she was a child, was already imagining the house when it was restored.

Paula hid a sigh. So this is where Eddie had lived and died. Maybe he was even buried here. It was the kind of place that looked like it would have a family cemetery. If so, she would put flowers on his grave, as she'd forgiven him long ago. Sort of.

"Mom, look at the porch." Addie was pointing to a mammoth addition on the south side of the house. "Won't the boys love playing on that?"

"We'd better see what condition it's in first," Paula said, imagining splinters and rusty nails and trips to the emergency room of the local hospital, if there was such a thing.

But Addie was examining the key ring given to her by the round-faced lawyer. "I can't wait to see the inside. I think the front door key is this one."

"Go on," Paula said. "I'll get the boys and follow you in a minute." She turned to smile at her handsome grandsons. "You were very good boys today," she told them. "Grandma's gonna buy you some ice cream on the way home."

"Yay!" Ian shrieked, while Matthew was busy unbuckling his seat belt. Paula managed to get them out of the car, eventually, though she wondered when seat belts and car seats had gotten so damned complicated.

Addie was already inside, so Paula took each boy by the hand and led them up the stone steps to the wide porch.

"Is anybody home?" Matt wanted to know, peering through the open door.

"Is this a school?"

"No, this is a house, and no one lives here. Not right now." And, from the looks of the front hall, whoever lived here hadn't spent much money making it look nice. That answered the question of whether Eddie had ever married again.

"Mom?" Addie poked her head out from around a corner. "You have to see the parlor."

"I'm sure I do." She kept her grip on the boys' little hands and turned right, into a large room that looked as if it hadn't been occupied since Texas declared statehood. The light fixture, a Victorian marvel of glass and bronze, was the only thing in the room aside from an ornate woodstove with its chimney disappearing into the outside wall. The rest of the downstairs was similar—bare, dusty rooms with no furniture, and drapes hanging in shreds at the long windows. The floors were made of large pine boards, and the walls held fading floral paper. A large bathroom boasted pink and black tiles and a claw-foot tub. One room with a fireplace, that must have served as Eddie's living area, had a battered green recliner and a large television set.

"Your father sprung for cable," Paula said. "Imagine that."

"Well, we can see why he had money to buy land." Addie's hands were on her hips, and Matt leaned against her leg.

"I'm afraid to look in the kitchen."

"No kidding." Her daughter headed to a door that Paula guessed would lead to the Room From Hell. "Brace yourself."

"I'll breathe through my mouth." But she almost forgot to breathe at all when she entered the largest kitchen she'd ever seen. The room was an enormous rectangle, with a long counter, stove and sink lined up on two of the walls, along with two refrigerators that were probably older than Addie. A wide farm table dominated the room, surrounded by wooden chairs of various shapes and styles.

"It looks like something out of a magazine," Addie said, obviously meaning it as a compliment, from the awed look on her face. Paula decided not to comment, because Matt let go of her hand and climbed onto one of the chairs.

"Cool!" Ian followed him and the two of them sat at the large table grinning at the devoted women in their lives. "Is it lunchtime yet?"

"Who lives here?" Matt wanted to know, eyeing the hunting rifles mounted beside the back door.

"No one," his mother said, reaching for him. "Let's go upstairs and see what's there."

They had passed a wide staircase in the front hall, but a narrow set of stairs lay to the right of the back door. Paula followed the boys and Addie up the stairs to the second floor, which was hot and stuffy. She counted five bedrooms and one bathroom. Each bedroom had its own pedestal sink, as if the place had been an inn at one time.

Another set of stairs led to another hall with three more bedrooms and another bathroom, plus a narrow set of stairs Addie predicted led to an attic.

"We'll save the attic for another time," she said. "I just want to take it all in and picture myself living here."

Her mother blanched. "But you don't know anything about ranching."

"Who said it's going to be a ranch?"

"You just have to look around—cows, horses, barns, pastures. Spells 'ranch' to me."

"Well, I'm looking at eight bedrooms and a sun porch."

"And a money pit."

"Not if I do a lot of the work myself."

"What do you want with an eight-bedroom house?"

"A home," Addie replied, smiling so hard it was a wonder her face didn't break apart. "My father left me a home."

"I JUST GOT AN EDGY feeling, that's all," John muttered, stepping out of his old, blue pickup truck. He wiped his forehead and squinted against the sun. "Like a storm's coming."

Cal looked up at the sky. It was still as blue and cloudless as it had been this morning. "Maybe you drank too much coffee. You should cut back at your age, you know."

"Thanks for the advice, Doc, but I'm tellin' you, I'm having one of them premonitions, like trouble's coming and it's right around the corner."

"Maybe the lawyer's coming back to tell us the place is sold." Cal looked at his watch. "I've been up most of the night with the calving, John. I'm going to sit down for a while."

"You think you're going to have another long night?"

"Yeah. Wish we could hire more help right now." He yawned. He was tired, dirty and just about walking in his sleep. "There won't be any more days off until the calving's done."

"Don't worry about me," John said. "I'll keep up."

Cal shook his head. "You've got enough to do with the horses. But I'll let you know if I need help tonight."

Old John seemed content with that promise, so Cal headed toward his own small house, a two-room bunkhouse that at one time had housed the summer crew. Now it held a bedroom, living and kitchen area and a bathroom. Small, but all his. After growing up in group homes, where he owned nothing but a toothbrush and a bagful of secondhand clothes, Cal figured this old building was just about perfect.

He was asleep when the storm struck. The next thing he heard, through the fog of a thick, dreamless sleep, was Old John yelling about something.

"She's here!" the old man hollered. "She's here!"

"Who?" Cal couldn't have opened his eyes if someone had offered him a one-way ticket to a beach on Maui. He'd seen pictures of Hawaii, and often dreamed about it. *Palm trees,* he mused, *and pineapples the size of—*

"Get up! You got to get up right now!"

"I don't care who's here," Cal muttered. "I've been awake for twenty-five hours straight and I'm damn well going to—"

"Meet Ed's daughter," John finished for him. "She's here, and she's looking over the place, and she wants to meet the help."

Cal swore and tossed back the thin sheet.

"She's a pretty thing," the old man babbled. "Doesn't look anything like Ed, but she seems nice enough and real interested in the ranch, and she has two little boys, twins, cutest little tykes you've ever seen, look like they could give you a run for your money, all right, and—"

"John."

"Yeah?"

"Where is she?" Cal looked around for his jeans and grabbed them off the back of a wooden chair.

"In the big house, looking around. You should have seen her face when she was talking about that house, why, she couldn't believe it, I'll bet. And—"

"What about the husband?" He found a clean shirt and threw that on before he started on socks and boots. "What's he like?"

"Not here. She came with her mother."

"I'd like to meet the man I'm working for."

"Yeah, you and me both, son. But for right now it's the little lady and her mom, both of them lookers, all right, but the mother isn't real pleased with the Triple J, if you know what I mean."

Cal didn't, but he wasn't about to ask John for an explanation that would keep him talking all the way to the main house. "Where are they from?"

"Austin."

His eyebrows rose, and he slammed his Stetson on his head and headed for the door. "Guess they weren't a real close family."

"Son, you don't know the half of it," the old man muttered. But Cal didn't have time to ask him what he meant, because there in front of the house stood the yellow-haired woman who haunted his dreams and turned them into nightmares.

"Hello, there," was all he could think to say. She looked good, more *maternal* than he remembered. Her hair was still streaked with gold, but it curled around her face now. He liked her better without all that makeup, too, but he missed the low-cut top. She had a figure that could make men weep, but today she wasn't looking for someone to dance with or buy her a drink. Either this was his Valentine's Day woman or her twin sister. Behind her came an older woman hauling two little boys.

"Hello." She stepped closer and stuck out her

hand. "I'm Adelaide Larson." She cleared her throat. "Ed Johanson's daughter."

He took the small hand in his and remembered how those fingers felt upon his skin. "I'm Cal McDonald. Nice to finally meet you."

She withdrew her hand as quickly as was polite, but he saw the relief in those sky-blue eyes. Her cheeks were flushed, and she turned away to introduce her mother, a sharp-eyed fiftysomething version of Adelaide Larson. A woman who didn't miss much, he suspected.

"Mrs. Johanson," he said, noting that she didn't let go of the twins' hands. He'd bet those little boys were hell on wheels. He tipped his hat. "It's nice to meet you."

"Mr. McDonald."

"Call me Cal."

Adelaide Larson introduced her sons, who grinned up at him. One of them asked if he knew where the horses lived, and the other stared, wide-eyed, at John.

"I can show you the horses," Cal said. He looked up at the woman. "Your father bought a nice herd of mares about five minutes before he died."

"Were you there?"

"Neither one of us was," he told her. "It happened real fast."

"Oh."

At least she looked sad about it, he thought. John motioned to the twins. "Come here, you rascals. I'll take you to the horses, but only if you hold my hands."

"We're not babies," one of them said.

"Ian," his mother warned. "Watch your manners."

"You don't have to hold my hand," the old horseman said. "Just my thumbs." He showed them his huge, gnarled hands, out of which stuck two massive thumbs. Awed, the little boys did as they were told. Even the grandmother looked impressed, though she moved closer in case the old man slipped up and let one of those little guys loose.

"Mrs. Larson," Cal said, falling into step with the little blonde. She was married, he realized, noting the wedding band on her left hand that hadn't been there when they'd met nearly two months ago. "What are you and your husband planning to do with the ranch?"

"What?" She'd grown pale, and she looked at him as if he'd said something in a foreign language.

"The ranch," he repeated. "Will you keep it, sell it, run it yourselves?" He didn't make love to other men's wives. And he didn't think much of women who hid their wedding rings and went to bars with their girlfriends.

"I'm not sure." She walked faster, obviously

anxious to keep up with her children. And avoid any private conversation with the man she'd slept with. Cal hid his disappointment over that wedding ring. Here he'd hoped that he'd meet her again someday—he'd gone to Billy's to look for her every Saturday night for four weeks after Valentine's Day. He'd spent way too many hours wondering who she was and what he'd say if he ever saw her again.

He hadn't forgotten that lonely look in her eyes. It was still there, meaning her husband wasn't good enough for her. No woman that pretty should look so painfully sad. But he'd forgotten for a moment that she'd just lost her father. Maybe that's where the sadness came in. Maybe her husband brought her flowers and rubbed her back and told her she was beautiful.

He'd like to meet the sorry son of a bitch.

LUCK HAD PLAYED A TRICK on her once again. Addie kept her eyes on her kids, attached to the old cowboy and heading toward a gray barn and a large corral several hundred yards away. The boys tried to step in mud puddles, but John, who wasn't interested in using last names, managed to avoid the mud. He seemed like he knew his way around children.

Her mother kept an eye on all three of them,

though she walked slower and looked around the place as if she couldn't believe it was real. And Addie, chin up and shoulders back, carried on as if she and the tall ranch hand had never met each other before this morning, though she could feel him watching her.

She was, literally, a walking disaster. She had gotten married to a man she loved, had healthy twin sons and then—whammo—her husband died. She goes out for the first time in three years, ends up making love to a handsome cowboy and what happens? She gets pregnant, or at least she was about seventy-five percent sure she was. Inherits a ranch. Discovers the man she had a one-night stand with and hoped never to see again *works* on the property.

It wasn't fair. Wild Kate had affairs all the time and never looked back, never crossed that invisible line into disaster, never so much as had to buy a pregnancy test kit and watch the stick turn color.

Cal McDonald looked as if he hadn't slept in days, and hadn't shaved, either. He had dark circles under his eyes and that scruffy appearance that sold underwear in magazine ads, and yet he still looked good. And there was still that unsettling sizzle between them. Or maybe that was guilt, she wondered. But what was the odd, comforting feeling she recognized once again? And why would she have the same reaction, without having had a rum and Coke since February fourteenth?

"Mrs. Larson," he said again, as if he needed to remind her that she was married. He thought she had cheated on her husband, of course.

"Call me Adelaide. Or Addie."

"Mrs. Larson," he repeated, walking next to her, just a little too close. "I'm really sorry about your father."

"Thank you."

"I didn't know he had any family."

"In other words, where on earth was his daughter all this time?" She stopped, and he did, too. They stood there looking at each other for a long moment.

"No, ma'am," he drawled. "Your family relations are none of my business."

"I haven't seen my father since I was two," Addie explained, unwilling to let this man think she was a bad daughter, as well as an unfaithful wife. "He walked out on my mother and me and we never heard from him again, not until a lawyer tracked us down a few days ago."

"I'm sorry." She almost believed him. They started walking again. She heard the boys chattering to the old man and knew they were soaking up a man's attention.

"How long have you worked here?"

"A little more than twenty years."

"Are you the boss?"

"I run the cattle operation. John pretty much works with the horses. Your father was the boss."

"Is there anyone else here?" She stopped before reaching the corral, where the boys gazed at a beautiful, chestnut horse that had approached the fence.

"We hire some extra hands in the summer. But John and I are the only ones who live here permanently. Your father wasn't much for spending money on the help."

"I gathered that. He didn't spend money, period. I take it you've been inside the house?"

"Just in the kitchen. And only once in the rest of the place. Ed kept to himself, and conversations about the operation were confined to the kitchen in the big house, or John's place." He hesitated, and Addie waited. "You said you didn't know what you were going to do with this place, but whatever it is, keep in mind that John's close to eighty. I'm not sure where he'd go if he had to leave."

"No one is going to be forced to leave," Addie said, horrified to think that he'd assume she'd toss an old man out of his home. "Unless he wants to."

Cal frowned and looked away, past the horse barn with the peeling white paint, past the corrals filled with beautiful horses, before turning back to look down at her. "I don't sleep with other men's wives."

"Good for you." She gave him what she hoped was an innocent smile. He'd learn the truth soon enough, but she didn't feel like discussing her personal history with a man who'd seen her naked in a cheap motel.

4

Cal sat on his bed and pulled off his boots for the second time in one afternoon. He was going to quit the Triple J. He'd give his two weeks' notice, pack up his truck and leave, just like that. He wasn't about to work for a man whose wife he'd slept with. And he wasn't about to forget that night in the motel, either, even if he hadn't known she was married at the time.

And he wasn't about to stop wanting Addie Larson. Which was the biggest problem of all. He stood, stripped off his clothes and headed for a hot shower and a few hours' sleep before another night spent in the calving shed began.

Damn. She was prettier than he'd remembered. Softer. Sweeter. He wouldn't have pictured her a mother, but today he saw that she was a good one. She watched those two kids to make sure they didn't get into anything that could hurt them, and she made them mind their manners, too. He'd heard more than one "Yes, please," and "No, thank you."

Neither one had mentioned their father, though. Cal had listened to their chatter all the way from the horse barn to the calving pens and back to the main house. They'd stayed two hours and it felt like the Larsons had been there for two days. No one on the Triple J was used to company. Ed, hermit that he was, hadn't encouraged visitors. John had no family that he ever spoke of, though he'd mentioned being married once. And there sure were no McDonalds coming to say hello and staying for coffee.

Once Cal was clean he opened a beer and, wearing boxers and a T-shirt, stretched out on his bed, his head supported by three pillows.

"Hey, Calvin!" John was the only person who used his full name.

"Yeah?"

"You asleep yet?"

"Take a wild guess!" he hollered, and then he heard the door open and the old man shuffle inside. John stopped when he saw Cal spread out on his cot.

"What's the matter with you?"

"Nothing. Why?"

"You don't seem real happy."

"Should I be?"

"Well, hell, yes. We got ourselves a real pretty boss and she doesn't seem anxious to change anything. I'm happy. I'm gonna celebrate and make up a batch of enchiladas. You want to join me?"

"Now?"

"Hell, no, not now. Suppertime. At six." He looked at his watch, a timepiece so scratched and worn it was a miracle John could see the time. "Four hours from now."

"Sounds good." Cal yawned, then took another swallow of beer. "Help yourself," he told the man. "Nice and cold."

"No, thanks. I just came over to tell you that Miss Addie called on her cell phone and said she'd be moving into the house in a couple of weeks. Asked me some questions about the house and the plumbing and all that."

"And you knew the answers?" He got out of bed and followed John back into the kitchen. So it was "Miss Addie" now, and not "Mrs. Larson."

"Nah. But I told her just to call me anytime and I'd do what she wanted."

"What about the husband?" He pretended to be casual, going so far as to open the refrigerator and offer the old man a Mountain Dew, which was John's favorite drink. "What did you hear about him? Divorced?"

"She was wearing her wedding ring, Cal," he said, taking the can. "Thanks. Her mom told me that that poor girl's husband died a few years ago, when those kids were little."

"*Died?*"

"Yeah. In a car accident. I'm surprised Ed didn't say anything about that." John pulled up a chair and sat down at the table that was barely big enough for two people.

"How would he know?"

John shrugged. "I got a feeling he kept track."

"Imagine that." Cal leaned against the counter and wondered why he felt so damn pleased with life all of a sudden. He should be afraid. Very afraid. Adelaide Larson wasn't married after all. She was a widow. She was available. And she was coming to live on the Triple J.

He knew now that this surely meant trouble. Widows with children wanted husbands. And he couldn't be called husband material, not by any stretch of the imagination. If Adelaide Larson didn't stay on her part of the Triple J, Cal knew he'd have to pack up and get out.

PAULA WAS ALMOST AFRAID to ask, but since she already suspected the answer, she went ahead. There were still thirty minutes left to drive before arriving home, after all, and Addie had been on the cell phone when Paula returned to the car with the promised ice cream. Now the boys were asleep in their car seats and the car was blessedly quiet. "You're going to live there, aren't you?"

"Of course." Addie smiled, something she had

done a lot today. It had to do with the house, an architectural accomplishment back in the 1890s, but an enormous drain of time and money today. Fortunately, her daughter had both. Or would, as soon as some of the property was sold. And she was certain Addie would waste no time taking care of that problem. Addie was good at problems. How else could she have taken care of things so well after Jack died? But even Addie might be biting off more than she could chew with that giant of a house.

"You know, it needs a lot of work," she felt it necessary to point out.

Addie laughed, another miracle. "Yes. That's the best part. I now have the time and the money and the house. What could be better?"

"And the ranch?"

"Will go on being a ranch."

"With John and Cal working for you, I assume, since you don't know anything about cows," Paula added, but Addie didn't respond for long moments.

"I guess," was the only thing she said, which was surprising. Paula thought her daughter had gotten along well with both men, and seemed pleased with the condition of the animals and the care of the buildings.

"What do you mean, you *guess*?"

"Meaning I don't know. Mr. McDonald might not want to stay."

"How formal you've become. He's a very good-looking man," Paula pointed out.

"I suppose," Addie said. "If you like that type."

"That type?" Paula chuckled. "You mean big, handsome and polite? Are you blind?" And it was about time Addie started noticing such things; the girl couldn't raise those boys alone. They needed a father, and Addie needed a man. And something told her that her daughter was well aware of Cal McDonald's sex appeal.

"Mom." It was said in the tone Addie used to warn her mother that she should stop talking. Paula didn't have any intention of stopping now, though.

"John told me that Cal has lived on the ranch for twenty years, almost as long as John has. And that Cal is one of the best cattlemen in the county. He said he's trustworthy and honest, too."

"Well, he can be as honest and trustworthy as he wants," she said, looking embarrassed, which Paula thought odd. And interesting. "As long as he doesn't interrupt my getting the house restored. I'm not sure I'm going to keep the animals, anyway."

"You just said—"

"For now, Mom. I won't make any changes for *now*."

"That's good," Paula said, noting the stubborn tilt to her daughter's chin. "Because if you're intent on moving into that old monstrosity of a house, you're going to need all the help you can get."

SHE'D SEEN HIM AGAIN and she hadn't died of embarrassment. That had been one accomplishment for the day, Addie decided. She dropped her mother off at her condominium, in an elegant, gated community just south of Round Rock, where her mother lived among other fifty-somethings in an oasis of swimming pools, hot tubs and tennis courts. She promised she would call her in the morning, promised she would let her know what she could do to help with the move, promised not to rush into any hasty decisions and also promised that she would try to get a good night's sleep. Yes, she'd promised, she would *think* about having a glass of wine before bed, just to make sure she would sleep.

And then she'd taken the boys to the grocery store, where they splurged on frozen pizza, root beer and cookies—tonight's supper. She also bought three more boxes of saltine crackers and two bottles of ginger ale, just in case tomorrow morning brought another queasy spell. She also managed to grab every decorating and remodeling magazine on the racks at the checkout stand, mostly for inspiration but also to cover the pregnancy test kit lying on the bottom of the shopping cart.

She'd seen him, she thought again later, after the boys were fed and sleeping, and no doubt dreaming of the horseback rides the old cowboy had promised them on their next visit to the ranch. She'd seen the man who had carried her across two parking lots and a field to take her to bed. A bed from which she'd run as soon as passion cooled and she'd realized what she'd done.

Addie skipped the wine and fixed peppermint tea instead. She took a notebook, her magazines and her father's bank statements to bed with her. She would make lists, she would add figures, she would stop thinking about the pregnancy test and the man who'd reappeared in her life today.

Call house inspectors, she wrote. She needed someone to go over the house and tell her what needed to be repaired or replaced.

Find repairmen who work in Nowhere. Waco was closer than Austin, so she might have to look there.

Get Waco phone book.

Quit job. That would be a joy. She'd managed to make the insurance settlement from Jack's death stretch by working evenings for a cleaning company. She cleaned offices from six to ten, four nights a week, while the teenager in the next apartment took care of the twins and put them to bed.

Decide what property to sell. A real estate agent should be able to give her advice. Kate might know someone reliable.

Call Kate. She'd already told her best friend about her father's will. Kate had listened to her guilty confession about the forty minutes at the motel, given her a tissue and a hug and welcomed her to the "weird world of dating." She'd hold off telling her about the reappearance of Motel Man, though. With any luck, he'd ride off into the sunset and she'd never have to face him again.

Buy Mom a new car. Addie knew exactly what her mother wanted, too. That was an easy one to take care of.

Decide what to take to Nowhere. If anything. The boys' beds would go, as would their toys and bookshelves. She would pack up the kitchen things, but the furniture wasn't worth moving. She would keep the Oriental rug her mother had given her, and she would bring her china and crystal, those rarely used wedding gifts that would finally have a place of honor in a dining room. She and Jack had been saving for a house before the twins were born, so the wedding china hadn't seen the light of day for years.

Take test. Pray. She would read the directions before she went to sleep. Tomorrow would be The Day. And she would deal with whatever the little stick displayed.

Keep clothes on. Addie crossed that one off as soon as she wrote it, then went back to scribble over it so it couldn't be read. Her reaction to Cal's presence was anything but sane. One look at the man and she wanted to press herself against him and feel those strong arms wrap around her. She wanted that warmth again, that feeling of being wanted and possessed. Irrational, yes. She was a woman with responsibilities and a code of behavior that didn't jibe with one-night stands.

Decide on a moving day. The sooner the better. Addie leaned against her pillows and closed her eyes. She might have never known her father, but he had given her and her sons a chance at a wonderful new life, and for that she was very, very grateful.

No matter what happened.

So the next morning, while the boys were eating cereal and watching cartoons on television, Addie watched the pregnancy test results and learned that she was going to have a baby.

So much for condoms. And just her luck to have been on the receiving end of a defective one, which must have been what had happened. Surely a man Cal's age knew how to use one properly. He'd had all the other moves down pat. Her body had responded to every touch and caress, every passionate moment.

She nibbled on crackers and sipped ginger ale, all the while wishing she could tolerate a strong cup of black coffee. She needed caffeine, and she needed to decide how she would handle having a baby without a husband. Women did it all the time, she realized, but that didn't mean it was easy. Raising Ian and Matt without a father was the hardest thing she'd ever done in her life. But she could do it again. Especially now that she didn't have to worry about money, and she had a home, a *real* home, to give her children.

Maybe this child would be a girl. Addie thought of pink dresses and lace-ruffled socks, hair bows and pastel blankets. And then she thought of her burgeoning stomach—surely she'd be showing in about three or four months—and what Cal would think. Would she tell him? Maybe she wouldn't have to. Maybe he'd be long gone by the time she started looking like there was a basketball under her shirt and he could put two and two together and come up with "father."

She would wait. She had plenty of time. There were more immediate problems, such as when she would tell her mother. And exactly *what* she would tell her mother. *I was abducted by horny aliens. I used a sperm donor and a turkey baster. I had wild sex with a stranger on Valentine's Day.*

Paula would believe none of it.

"WHO JUST LEFT?" CAL WATCHED John walk across the yard from the main house.

"Cleaners." The old man grinned. "It took them four days, but that old house is shining for the first time in a long time."

"I thought I saw a furniture truck." Cal didn't know where Adelaide Larson got her money, but she sure as hell could spend it.

"Yeah. I let them in about an hour ago. Some beds came, and a washer and dryer. I thought there'd be more, but I guess Miss Addie is going to wait 'til the house is fixed up before she buys more new stuff."

"They still moving in today?" He shoved his hands in his pockets and tried to look casual, but John gave him one of those eagle-eyed stares, as if he knew that Cal had ironed his shirt and taken extra care shaving this morning.

"Yeah. Should be any time now."

"I guess I'd better get back to work," he said, but he didn't move. She would be living only a few hundred yards away. He wished he knew more about her. Was she a Saturday night party girl who made a habit out of picking up men in bars? Somehow he doubted it. But if he'd learned one thing about women in his nearly forty years, it was that you couldn't tell by looking at one what they were like. The quiet ones could fool a man, all right.

"Stick around," John said. "She's going to need our help."

"She's going to need a *lot* of help," Cal pointed out, gazing at the peeling old Victorian, with its gables and peaked roof, its north addition and the wide porch that ran along the front and one side. He hoped for Addie's sake that it was sturdy and worth the trouble to fix it up, if that's what she really wanted to do.

"That's why she's got us." John winked at him.

"We're not carpenters. Just painting the outside of that house is going to be a full-time job. I hope she can afford it."

"I wouldn't worry about that. The mother told me that Ed left his daughter 'nicely settled' in his will. 'Nicely settled,' that's how she put it."

"You and Mrs. Johanson are talking a lot?"

"We keep in touch. She's been helping Miss Addie get things organized." John kicked a clod of dirt. "Anyway, she said not to worry about the ranch, that her daughter could afford to run it, least for a while."

"Well, that's a relief." Maybe. He still wasn't sure if he would stick around. "Who'd have thought that Ed had two pennies to rub together?"

"He was an odd duck, all right," the old man

declared. "But he was good to me, and he didn't have much reason to be." John's lined face broke into a smile. "Here they come, son. Hang on to your hat, cuz life's about to change!"

"Like that's news?" Cal quipped, having thought about those changes for the past two weeks, ever since he'd seen Adelaide Larson for the second time in his life.

Sure enough, three cars came up the driveway, clouds of dust trailing in their wake. The sky was bright blue, and the sun beat down with the scorching intensity of July, not April. Adelaide Larson had herself a hot day to move into her new home, but Cal suspected she wouldn't let it bother her. He'd seen her from a distance before today; she'd carried a clipboard and a measuring tape. Sunglasses hid her eyes and a wide, straw hat covered her hair, and sometimes she talked into a cell phone. He had the feeling she was going to make things happen here on the Triple J. She'd been here several times in the past two weeks and she hadn't sought him out, so he guessed she didn't have any questions about the cattle operation.

Or she was avoiding him. Which was just fine.

He watched the cars come to a stop. Someone honked a horn when John lifted a gnarled hand in greeting. The boys tumbled out the back door of Addie's old station wagon, at the same time a tall brunette—Cal thought she might be the same woman he'd seen Addie with at Billy's—climbed out of a black SUV. Mrs. Johanson opened the driver's side door of a new, red Chevy pickup. Hopping down, she called something to Addie, who by now stood in the driveway and watched the little boys chase each other around the old soap kettle on the front lawn. She wore khaki shorts and a black tank top that raised Cal's temperature another ten degrees.

"Looks like we've been invaded," he muttered to John, but the old man had already headed toward the women. Cal hesitated. He watched the kind of family scene of which he had no part and felt like he was ten years old again, on the outside looking in. It was the kind of thing that made him want to turn on his heel and head in the opposite direction so he wouldn't have to feel so bad. He was fine, Cal assured himself. Going on forty and perfectly content.

Except in times like this. He couldn't walk away, though. Not with three women and one old man unloading boxes from the back of the pickup. He had no choice but to start moving toward them.

"Hey! Mr. Cal!" One of the little boys waved to him and started running in his direction. The other boy was just about ready to go headfirst into the kettle, but Cal didn't think there was anything that could hurt him. It should have held flowers, but Ed hadn't been much for spending money on things that weren't absolutely necessary.

Cal caught the kid before he plowed into his abdomen. "Hi, there," he said. "Which one are you?"

Brown eyes stared up at him. "I'm Ian. You can't tell, can you?" He didn't wait for an answer. "Mom said we hafta call you Mr. Cal because that's polite."

"Well, you have to do what your mother says." Cal figured that was a safe enough answer.

"Yeah." The boy grabbed Cal's hand and tugged him toward the driveway. The little hand around Cal's fingers was warm and very soft. "My gramma got a new truck and I got to pick it out. And my mom says that Matt and me get our own rooms, but we like sleepin' together so we said no and she said okay."

"Sounds like a plan."

"Sounds like a plan," the boy repeated, clearly thrilled with the phrase. "Yeah, sounds like a plan." He walked Cal right to his mother, who smiled politely and said hello, before he ran off to join his twin in the grassy section of the front yard.

"Hello," was the only brilliant thing Cal could think to say. He lifted the large cardboard box out of her arms and pretended he didn't notice that his fingers had grazed the bare skin of her arms. She smelled like vanilla and roses, a scent he remembered from that night. Her skin was pale, and there was a fragile look to her that surprised him.

"Thanks." She gave him a quick smile and didn't meet his gaze. Clearly she was as uncomfortable with him as he was with her. And neither one of them could forget that night. She quickly introduced her friend Kate, whose arms were full of bedding. "Kate, this is Cal McDonald. He works here with John."

"Nice to meet you," the brunette said, her eyes twinkling with mischief. "You look familiar. Have we met before?"

"Kate," Addie said, darting a look at her mother to see if she was listening. Paula was deep in conversation with John, while the twins had turned their energy into walking up and down the front porch steps. "Don't."

"I'm sorry." She laughed and shook her head. "I'll behave. Where do you want these sheets and blankets? And when do I get a tour of this mansion?"

"Right now." Addie picked up another box from the back of the truck and headed across the lawn to the front door. "You won't believe the foyer. Or how many rooms there are. Follow me and prepare to be amazed."

Cal followed behind Kate, but his gaze was on

the little blonde ahead of her. There were ten or twenty reasons why the woman was off-limits, and yet the vision of her naked and against his body wouldn't go away.

He was only human.

And he obviously needed to get off the ranch more often.

5

"WHERE DO YOU WANT IT?"

Addie turned and saw Cal standing in the doorway of her new bedroom. He held the ornate, white iron headboard she'd bought in Austin last week, along with new beds for the house and other extravagant necessities. She'd splurged on a king-size mattress, too, which leaned against one of the walls. Now, with Cal walking into her bedroom, she thought the size of the bed could be misconstrued. *I'll be sleeping here alone,* she wanted to say. *I have no ulterior motives, and will be sending out no invitations.*

She really wished someone else could put her bed together, but there was nothing to do but accept the fact that Cal was here and prepared to help. And she needed all the help she could get. So she pointed to the large expanse of wall between the two east windows. "Over there, thanks."

He carried it inside, making sure he lifted it above the freshly scrubbed wooden floor, and set it against a faded pink wall that was destined for new wallpaper. He made another trip, but not alone. Kate carried the other end of the pair of bed frames.

"That's one heck of a formal staircase," she said, panting a little after setting the frame down in the middle of the room. "You can make quite a grand entrance."

"It is dramatic, isn't it? Especially with the chandelier hanging down from two stories. Like something in a magazine."

Kate nodded. "Exactly. Too bad you only have sons. This would be a great place to get married."

"You're welcome to use it anytime," Addie teased, knowing full well her friend wasn't interested in settling down. Cal went over and scooted the bed frame into position.

"I might surprise you." Kate turned to look at the cowboy. "Hey, Cal? Do you need me anymore?"

"No, but thanks for the help."

"Anytime." She winked at him and laughed in Addie's direction. "I haven't decided which one of the guest rooms up here is mine. Any suggestions?"

"There are three on the other side of the stairs, so take your pick. I've taped color swatches in each room for the painters, if color means anything to you. The one farthest back has the twin beds, and the other two are queens."

"Okay. Good luck with the bed, you two. I'm going back to the kitchen. Your mother and I are bonding over cooking equipment and the organization of your pantry."

"The fun never stops," Addie said. "I'll pay you back with dinner. What are the boys doing?"

"John took them for a walk. He's an old sweetie, that one." And then Kate was gone, leaving Addie alone with Cal again. She would have to learn to be comfortable around him, she decided. There was no other choice, not for right now. Not unless one of them left the Triple J.

"So," she said, sounding determinedly cheerful. "Can I help you with that?"

He didn't look up from tightening the bolts that held the metal frames together and also connected the headboard. "No."

"Okay." She felt a trickle of perspiration run down her back. She would have this house air-conditioned if it took every last dime of her inheritance. The room, large as it was, felt stuffy and close in April. What would it be like in August?

"I'm almost done."

"No hurry," she lied, taking a sip from the water bottle she'd left on top of the pine dresser, the one article of furniture she'd brought from her Austin bedroom. She'd finished filling the drawers with her clothes and had set a framed photo of Jack on top, along with the boys' baby pictures.

"Are we going to get to know each other, Addie, or are we just going to keep pretending we're strangers?"

She turned to face him. He tucked his wrench in his back pocket and went over to one of the box springs. The salesman had explained that twin frames held twin box springs, over which was placed her padded king-size mattress. "We already know each other a little too well."

His eyebrows rose. "After a few dances and half an hour in a motel room? I don't think so."

"Four dances and twenty minutes," she countered, "including my sprint across the parking lot."

Cal smiled, a fleeting smile that lightened his face for one brief minute as he slid the box spring along the floor. "At least I know your name now. You left without telling me."

"I didn't know yours, either."

"Stupid of me." Somehow he managed to make lifting the mattress look easy as he placed it on the frame. He was a large, muscular man. She remembered the strength in his arms when he'd carried her to the motel. She must have been insane to drink that much. The thought of all that rum made her stomach heave.

"What else do you want to know?" Damn, but

it was hot in this room. "There really isn't much else to say."

"How about why you ran away?" He walked closer to her, but stopped a few feet away, as if he was afraid she would run away again if he came too close.

She swallowed. Hard. "I was embarrassed. I don't expect you to believe me, but I, uh, had never done anything like that before. I was absolutely mortified."

"Mortified," he repeated, his dark eyes fixed on hers. "That's not very flattering."

"Well, you'll have to get compliments from the next woman you meet at Billy's. I'm sticking with 'mortified.'"

Again, that smile. "Well, no one's ever called it that before."

"It" meant sex, she supposed. Hot, panting, baby-making sex. Her stomach fluttered with nerves and more than a little guilt, but she kept quiet and hoped that the heat wasn't making her sick. Cal turned around and went back for the other box spring. He didn't say anything else until he had that one in place.

"You didn't tell me about your husband," he said, wiping his forehead with the sleeve of his shirt. "When you were here at the ranch that first day, you could have told me."

"I don't like talking about Jack's death."

"I'm sorry. I wouldn't have asked about him that day if I'd known." He watched her, waiting for her to say something.

"That's okay. It was three years ago." Three years and two months.

"That's not necessarily a long time."

"No," she said. "It's not."

"I'm sorry."

"Thank you." They looked at each other for a long moment before he stepped away.

"I think you're going to have to help me with this one," he said, moving toward the huge mattress.

"Let me get Kate." Heavy lifting and pregnancy didn't go together, and as long as she'd been given this baby she was going to do her best to keep it safe. "I have a bad back."

"Wait a sec. I'll see how far I get," Cal said, sliding it across the room. "Maybe I can manage by myself." His reluctance to take advantage of an excuse to be with Kate again pleased her. If he were immune to her friend's charms, he would set a record as the first man in Texas able to resist.

"Just a minute," she said, hurrying over to the shopping bag filled with new bedding. "I have to put the dust ruffle on first." She opened the package to reveal the almost transparent white nylon flocked with tiny pale green leaves. She gave it a good shake and told herself that the wrinkles would fall out eventually, because she wasn't going to stop and iron all that fabric.

To her surprise, he leaned the mattress against the wall and helped her spread the nylon square across the box springs as if he knew exactly what he was doing. When it was in place, Cal grasped the mattress again.

"Don't hurt yourself." A silly thing to say, of course, considering the size of him. She watched him manage to toss part of the mattress on top of the bed and push it into place. It didn't look easy and she heard him swear under his breath, but when she tried to help by grabbing one of the cloth handles on the side of the mattress, he told her not to.

"I'll take care of that," he said, his voice gruff. "But this is one hell of a big bed."

She flushed and stammered, "The boys sometimes get in bed with me in the morning."

"You don't have to explain," he said. "Your bed's your own business." Addie stayed silent while he pushed the mattress into place. It took several attempts, but Cal had it fixed in no time.

"Thank you. That's great." Now he could leave and she, ungrateful liar that she was, could admire her bed without thinking of sex.

"No problem," he said, looking up at her. "You have sheets for this?"

"Well, yes." They were still in their packages in the shopping bag in the far corner of the room, along with new pillows, a mint-green cotton blanket and a snow-white matelesse coverlet.

"Well, let's get 'em on, then. Might as well finish what we started."

He surprised her again, shaking the crisp, white sheets from their packages and spreading them neatly, tucking and folding with practiced motions.

"You're very good at this." He'd been married, of course, despite what he'd told her the night they met. He was older than she was—thirty-six, thirty-seven, she guessed—and he wouldn't have reached that age without having been someone's husband or live-in boyfriend, a man who'd grown accustomed to making beds. Who she was and what had happened was none of her business, Addie told herself.

"I did a lot of it when I was a kid."

"You did?" So much for the ex-wife.

"Yeah." He smoothed the blanket and folded the top edge neatly over the sheet. Addie did the same thing on the right side of the bed. "I spent most of my life in group homes. We made up our own beds every Sunday, and the older kids always helped the younger ones."

"And you were one of the older ones?"

"Younger, older, in between." He shrugged and

reached for the puffy plastic bag with the coverlet zipped inside. "This goes on top?"

"Yes." She was afraid to ask anything about his family, afraid to embarrass him or make him feel badly. And she didn't know if it would be rude to say nothing. She gazed at him across the width of the bed. "But where was your family?"

"There wasn't any." He gave her a quick smile, as if to reassure her that she shouldn't pity him, but the smile wasn't the same one that lit up his eyes when he was amused. She knew that much about him, at least. "Pillows?"

"Oh. Sure." She grabbed another shopping bag, this one stuffed with thick, down pillows, another splurge for all of the new beds in the house. She had spent one entire morning, while the boys were at preschool, in the bed and bath shop. She'd discovered that oyster crackers were more portable and less messy than the other kind, and were easily nibbled on while spending great quantities of money.

Which brought her back to the reason for the crackers in the first place, the man standing across the bed. The man who had used a condom. Had the damn thing broken?

"Addie?"

"Oh." She'd been staring at him. He walked around the bed and took the bag of pillows from her. "Sorry."

"Are you okay? You look a little pale."

"I'm fine. Just a little warm, that's all." Just a little pregnant, too. What would happen if she told him? No, she wasn't going to involve him. Not yet. Not until she knew what kind of man he was.

He looked up to the ceiling, where an ancient overhead fan hovered. "I wonder if that thing works."

"I don't know."

"Only one way to find out." He stepped around her and managed to reach the broken cord. In a matter of seconds, the wooden blades began to move, lifting the warm air toward the ceiling. "Better?"

"Yes, thank you."

"I'll tie a longer cord on it for you." But he wasn't looking at the fan when he spoke. His gaze was on her face. "I'll, uh, do that right away."

"Thank you," she managed. "Again."

"Again," Cal murmured, now looking at her mouth. He still held the bag of pillows, looking for all the world like a satisfied cowboy shopper, but his free hand reached out and touched her face. Addie didn't move, didn't dare breathe. She didn't want him to touch her, and yet she yearned for nothing more than to step into his arms. A kiss would be hell and heaven and a complete disaster, but she foolishly wanted nothing else. He had a beautiful mouth, and she knew what it felt like against her lips, against her skin, against her body.

His fingers swept slowly across her cheek, to her jaw, then moved to the side of her neck. She shivered and, looking as unsettled as she was certain she did, he dropped his hand.

"I should be—what was it? Oh, yeah. Mortified," he declared, but his mouth curved into a smile as he looked into her eyes. "But I wish I could carry you over to that bed and make love to you again. Longer this time," he said. "And more than once."

Addie took a deep breath and held his gaze with her own. "That's not going to happen."

"No," he said. "You're right. Things have changed, haven't they?" He didn't wait for an answer, simply tossed the bag of pillows onto the mattress and moved toward the bedroom door as if he wanted to get away from her as soon as he could. "The house looks good all cleaned up. Your father lived in a couple of rooms downstairs. I've never been up here before."

"Really?" She supposed it was only polite to give him a tour, and she was grateful to change the subject from making love to the condition of her new home.

"Too bad Ed never made the most of this place." He put his hands in his jeans pockets and looked around. "How many rooms are up here?"

"Well, this is mine, of course." She waved toward the curved windows at one end of the large rectangular space. "I couldn't resist that rounded wall. And there are three more bedrooms and two bathrooms on the other side of the hall, but those will be guest rooms."

"You must be expecting a lot of company."

"Maybe." If she ever needed the extra money, she could turn the house into a bed-and-breakfast.

"What about the boys?"

"Follow me." She led him to the other end of the room and through a door to a large bathroom, a room she intended to remodel as soon as possible. Some of the black-and-white tiles were cracked, and the old linoleum floor was peeling in places, but the wide claw-foot tub and elegant pedestal sink more than made up for the room's problems. "The master bathroom, obviously."

"Pretty fancy bathroom for an old ranch house. Makes you wonder who the original owners were."

"I wondered the same thing," she said. "Cattle barons, maybe?"

"You could look it up at the courthouse, I'll bet."

"Look at this." She led him into an enormous room that had intrigued her on the first visit. Empty except for the new twin beds, and boxes of the boys' clothing and toys, its tall windows let in lots of light and made the room a welcoming place for kids to play.

He whistled. "I never knew this room was up here."

"It's going to be the boys' playroom, but they'll sleep in here for now, until I get their bedrooms painted and fixed. I've ordered a rug, and once some shelves are installed, it should be perfect for them." At the end of the room, in the corner, was the back staircase. "We're right above the kitchen, so I'll be able to keep an eye on them."

"Yeah," he said. "I can see how that would be important."

Addie moved toward the staircase. "I'm going to fix some iced tea. Do you want some?"

"No, thanks. I'll go put the beds together in the other rooms."

"Okay." She didn't offer to help him, because she knew he'd refuse, and because she didn't want to be alone with him in other bedrooms and across other mattresses. He had wanted to kiss her, and she would have let him. And he would have known right away the power he had to make her knees weak and her heart pound against her chest. She was a silly, lonely, pregnant widow who should know better than to kiss the hired help.

And he was the kind of man who should know better than to try.

"MY ADELAIDE IS A WONDERFUL cook," Paula Johanson declared proudly. "I don't know where she got it from, because it certainly wasn't from me."

Cal watched the woman brush aside John's offers of help. She placed a large pan of steaming lasagna at the head of the table, where he assumed Addie would take her place once she finished putting food out. She'd insisted that everyone eat supper together tonight, but Cal would rather have bought a burger in town. He'd almost kissed her this afternoon. He'd stood in her bedroom, at the foot of that wide bed, and he'd touched her.

He didn't want to eat lasagna. He wanted a cold shower, a colder beer and a long, frigid drive in his air-conditioned truck.

"Well," John drawled, "if that lasagna tastes as good as it smells, you won't get no argument from me."

"No ar-gu-ment from me," one of the little boys repeated, grinning across the table at Cal. The boy seated next to Cal, the quieter one he thought was Matt, burst into giggles and covered his mouth with his hand.

"That'll be the day," his grandmother said. "You're *full* of arguments, Ian. And it's not polite to repeat people's words when they're speaking."

"Sorry," the boy mumbled, but he grinned at John as if the old man was his coconspirator.

"That's okay," John said, chuckling. The old man was in his glory with those kids around. Cal had never seen him so happy, not in years. Not even when Ed bought that Appaloosa mare and she'd given birth to one of the best-looking colts in the county.

"Thanks, everyone, for all of the help today," Addie said, sitting down at the head of the old farm table. John was on her left, Mrs. Johanson on her right. The twins sat opposite each other and, across from Cal, Kate lifted her wineglass.

"Here's to your new home, Addie," she said. "May you live here happily ever after."

"Thank you." She raised her glass and took a sip of water. Addie wasn't much of a drinker, he noted. Maybe Valentine's Day had put her off rum and Cokes for a while. Addie set her glass down and picked up a wide spatula. "I'm serving because it's too hot to pass around. John? Would you give me your plate? Help yourselves to salad and garlic bread."

Kate passed Cal the basket filled with hot bread. "When did you have the time to cook, Addie?"

"Yesterday. And then I packed the last of the kitchen stuff."

"Amazing," her friend said. "You're a true domestic goddess. You could make a fortune with your own restaurant, you know. With this table and your cooking—and these guys as waiters." She ruffled Ian's hair. "What a crew, huh?"

"I'd thought about a bed-and-breakfast," Addie said. "I've always wondered what it would be like. Maybe just on weekends, after the house is finished and the boys are in school. Cal? Would you give me your plate?"

"Sure, thanks." He looked at her as he leaned forward and gave his dinner plate to John to hold while Addie dished out a large chunk of lasagna. She was flushed, a little self-conscious and a whole lot pretty. And far away from the woman who had danced with him and laughed with him and reached for his shirt buttons two months ago.

"This *is* a wonderful table," her mother said. "You're going to keep it, aren't you, dear?"

"Yes."

Cal remained silent, except to thank John for the return of his plate piled with the best-smelling Italian food he'd ever had. He wasn't used to family dinners, though he'd always liked the old farm table. He figured it had served thousands of ranch hands over the many years it had sat in the middle of the room. The mismatched wooden chairs were a bit rickety, and he could understand if a woman didn't want to keep them. But the table? It had to be twenty feet long and four feet wide, and its battered surface gave it character. Like the old man sitting two chairs away, talking about the amount of stuff boxed and stacked in the storage rooms north of the kitchen.

"Your father never threw nothin' away." Sadness crossed the old man's face, and then he looked over at Addie and brightened. "He'd be real tickled that you were here taking care of everything."

"He should have looked me up in Austin," she said. "I would have been easy to find."

"Well, he wasn't a social man," John said. "More like a hermit, though maybe not that bad. The only time he'd leave here was when we'd go to a stock auction. And even then he wouldn't stay long, just do what business he came to do and then we'd leave. 'Cept that last time, of course. He wanted to buy them horses and just didn't live long enough to load them in the trailer."

"Them horses?" Ian asked. "How many horses?"

"It's a nice herd of eight mares," the old man answered, just as if the child knew what he was talking about. "Real nice mares. Six bays, a chestnut and a darn pretty paint pony that will make you a real good horse, there, boys, when you learn how to ride."

"Ride?" Matthew dropped his garlic bread. "Ride horses? Can we, Mom?"

"Maybe." Addie lifted the spatula. "Who would like more lasagna?"

"I want a horse," Ian said.

"Me, too," his brother added.

"You've got horses," said John. "'Course they're not good for learnin', no, not good for that." He leaned forward and looked down the table to Cal. "You'd better get these lads some ponies, Cal."

"That's up to their mother," he said, finishing the best lasagna he'd ever tasted. He helped himself to more Caesar salad and another slice of bread.

"Is there such a thing as *safe* ponies, Cal?" Addie's look said "tell me my boys won't get hurt" but Cal couldn't promise any such thing, of course.

"I can find some real mild ponies, sure. If the boys are going to grow up here on the Triple J, they should know how to ride."

Matt leaned over and gave him a big hug. "Thanks, Mr. Cal."

"You're welcome." Cal gave the boy an awkward pat and wondered what the hell he'd just promised.

"MY GOD, ADDIE, HE'S magnificent!" Since "he" had just left the kitchen after clearing the table and thanking Addie for supper, there was no doubt that Kate meant anyone but Cal McDonald. "Not classically handsome, of course, but very hot anyway. I think it's his eyes. Or those shoulders. Whatever. He's very, very hot, Addie. You lucky woman."

"Shh, my mother will hear you." She rinsed off another plate and set it in the drainer for Kate to dry. "She has ears like a hawk." .

"*Eyes* like a hawk, ears like a...what? A wolf? A cat?" Kate grinned.

"Fox," Addie said. "Ears like a fox, I think it is."

"Your mother is upstairs giving two noisy boys a bath. How on earth could she hear us whispering in the kitchen? This house is big enough for four families."

"I know." She smiled as she washed another plate. "I love it, don't you?"

"Well, it's a bit too witchy-gothic right now for me, but I can see that you're happy." Kate set the dry plate on the stack with the others. "Some wallpaper and paint will do wonders. And don't forget to call me when it's time to do some serious furniture shopping."

"I won't. I'd like a Victorian look, but without the dark wood." She eyed the kitchen cupboards, stained dark brown. "What color should I do the kitchen? I can't decide between blue and yellow."

"Red," Kate declared. "A nineteen-thirties deep red would look great with the wood in here. With white tile on the counters and red toile curtains and accents."

"Red toile," Addie repeated slowly, turning to survey the large room. "That could work."

"Very French country," Kate declared. "Very casual but elegant, in a ranchy kind of way without being ranchy, if you know what I mean."

"I think I do." Did she dare paint the cupboards red, or would the dark wood look okay if it was cleaned and waxed? She stopped washing and gazed upward, picturing the cupboards with white glass knobs instead of cast-iron handles.

"Now that we have that settled, let's talk about Cal. He is gorgeous and quite charming, in that 'strong, silent type' way. You said you actually *slept* with him that night? I mean, you didn't make that up or dream it or something?"

"Unfortunately, no. I mean, yes, I did—you know." She looked behind her at the door to what was now the family's living room. There was no sign of her mother or children lurking there, so she turned back to Kate. "I didn't stay there long. And I certainly didn't sleep. It was over…quickly."

Kate's eyebrows rose. "How very disappointing. Shame on him."

"No, it wasn't like that. We were both—" She

stopped, unwilling to share the intimate details, even with Kate.

"Satisfied?"

"Yes."

"Well, since you hadn't had sex in three years, I'm sure you were more than ready to be…satisfied. Quickly." Clearly Kate was willing to give Cal the benefit of the doubt there. "And then you grabbed your clothes and ran?"

"I put on my clothes—most of them—and ran. And he tried to catch up with me to ask my name—I told you that part already."

"But I want to hear it again. It's rather romantic."

"Sordid," Addie corrected. "It's rather sordid."

"Well, that depends."

"On what?"

"On what happens next. Are you going to slink around acting guilty and miserable, or are you going to 'satisfy' each other again?"

"Neither."

"Please tell me that you're not going to let that man go to waste? I'd give him a whirl myself, but he couldn't take his eyes off you all through dinner. He was practically drooling in his lasagna, you know."

"He wasn't."

"Trust me, Addie, honey, I know when a man wants a woman, and that man wanted you."

"He's not getting me," Addie declared, flushing under Kate's scrutiny. She would rather milk cows than tell her friend that Cal had almost kissed her this afternoon. And that she had wanted—for one brief crazy moment—to haul him across that new, wide mattress and kiss him senseless.

Her baby-growing hormones were definitely out of control.

And Addie, who had always prided herself on being an open and honest person, realized she had become frighteningly good at keeping secrets.

6

SHE THOUGHT SHE'D LOVE being alone in her new bed Saturday night. Her mother had gone to sleep an hour earlier in the former parlor that Ed Johanson had used as a bedroom. Paula had organized Ed's meager possessions, storing papers and photographs in boxes for Addie to browse through another day. They'd made up yet another one of the new beds.

And now the house was quiet, with Kate across the hall in what they called "the blue room," and the boys happily occupying the big room next door, sleeping like five-year-olds who'd just spent their first day on a ranch.

So Addie knew she should be content in her enormous bed, on crisp white sheets with a higher thread count than she'd known existed, her head resting on soft piles of goose down.

It was all too much, she thought, listening to the quiet whirring of the ceiling fan above her bed. Too many things had changed, even though most of the changes were good ones. She splayed her hands across her flat abdomen and wished she knew what to do with this particular change. Would Cal welcome the news of fatherhood? Would he be angry, and leave, never to be seen again, as her own father had when confronted with a family life he couldn't enjoy? And if he left, how would she run a cattle ranch?

John was too old to do much more than give advice. According to her father's will, he had the lifetime use of his little house and a small monthly salary to supplement his Social Security check. Something about a trust, the lawyer had explained, though at the time she'd missed some of the details.

Cal's salary had been paid for the next six months, another odd stipulation of her father's will. Perhaps Ed Johanson had meant for her to have the help she needed to run things here, but she knew nothing about horses or cattle except what they looked like. But, she decided, she could always hire someone else after the six months. Surely she could find another ranch hand or, if she had to, stop raising beef cattle. Maybe she could lease the cattle pastures, or whatever the land was called, to another ranch in the area. She would manage to think of something.

But maybe Cal would want to be a father.

Maybe he would demand his share of custody, and this baby would be in a crazy tug-of-war between two people who loved her. Or him. She pictured handing over her baby—wearing a pink dress and a ruffled hat—to Cal and his future girlfriends to care for on weekends and holidays and summer vacations. No, that was not going to happen. Not to her child.

She'd managed just fine without a father. She'd never hated the man or resented him for leaving. She'd actually spent her childhood thinking her father would drive up to the little house in south Austin and take her away to live with him in a house on the ocean or a castle in England. He would explain that he'd had amnesia, like Damon on her mother's favorite television show, and now that he had his memory back he would never leave his favorite little girl again.

Of course, the dreams never came true, but she had survived. And triumphed. Uncle Ned had given her away at her wedding, and she'd had Jack, who'd loved her for years and given her a family of her very own.

Cal had been a mistake. An unwilling sperm donor. A man she thought she'd never see again, until Mr. Anders had pulled out the map of Nowhere, Texas, and she realized that fate had decided otherwise.

She was not a lucky person, but right now, anyone who saw her would think she was the most fortunate person in Nowhere, at least. She was a woman of property. A woman who owned livestock and had two ranch hands and miles of fenced land.

But she would rather have had a father than his money.

Addie closed her eyes and rolled over on her side. She was a woman alone in a big bed and all she wanted to do was cry.

"CAN YOU TEACH ME ABOUT COWS?"

It was the last thing Cal expected Addie to say. But he hadn't expected her to knock on his door, either. He'd managed to avoid the woman for three days, and here she was, two minutes after he'd walked in the door after a long morning spent dealing with sick calves. And now he smelled worse than they had. So he wasn't prepared for company, not even when a pretty woman stood at his door.

"I need to know how the cattle business works," she said, staring up at him with barely disguised impatience. She held a stack of notebooks against her chest and she looked so serious, he wanted to laugh. But he didn't dare. "Can you explain it to me?"

"Why?"

"Oh, for heaven's sake!" Her blue eyes flashed. "Because, Cal, I'm *asking* you to."

He backed up and pushed the door open so she could step into his kitchen. She moved past him quickly, as if afraid to accidentally touch him, and he guessed he couldn't blame her. Whenever they were too close together, there were enough sparks between the two of them to burn down a barn.

"I meant," he drawled, once she was inside and standing by the small table, "why are you asking *me*?"

"You're the expert," she said, looking up at him with those blue eyes that made him want to drop to his knees and beg her to go to bed with him. The thought of it made him smile, just a little. His little bed would never be the same if Addie Larson were in it with him.

"Quit laughing," she said, looking beautiful in a bright blue T-shirt and baggy tan shorts. The woman had a nice pair of legs, he remembered. And here they were in his bunkhouse. "I'm serious."

"I'd help you if I could, of course. But Ed kept his business operations to himself, Addie. He made all the decisions and I followed orders."

"Oh." She looked so disappointed, he felt sorry for her.

"Would you like a drink?" He opened the refrigerator to see what he could offer. "I have beer, iced tea and oh, yeah, a Mountain Dew. Or I can put on some coffee."

"Iced tea would be good." She set the battered notebooks on the table and sat down in the chair facing him. "Let me be honest," she began. He turned, a tray of ice cubes in his hand.

"All right," he said, wondering what the hell was coming next. When a woman wanted to be "honest," it was his experience that nothing good could come of the rest of the conversation. He filled a tall, plastic glass with ice and poured some cold tea over it, then set the glass on the table in front of her. "But after I get out of these clothes and take a shower."

"Do you have to?" She looked at her watch.

"Yeah," he said. He could delay this "honest" stuff for a few more minutes easily enough, and he wasn't going to be this close to Addie when he smelled like cow. "I have to. Where are the kids— with John?"

"No. I wouldn't do that to him. They're at a prekindergarten session in town. And I have an appointment at two-thirty."

"I'll be quick," he promised. And he was as good as his word, too, showering in record time and, dressed in clean jeans and one of his best shirts, returning to the kitchen in less than ten minutes. He was barefoot and his hair was wet, but he didn't think Addie would care. She was ready to talk business and have some kind of honest discussion with her ranch hand, that was all. She hadn't come to unbutton his shirt or tell him to make love to her.

"Wow, that was fast." Addie had spread the notebooks across the table and had drunk half of her tea. She had a pen in her hand and a small calculator on top of one of the notebook's pages.

"I've learned to be quick, before the hot water runs out." He refilled her tea and fixed a glass for himself before sitting down across from her. "So, what's the problem?"

She stared at him for a long moment—so long, he wondered if she'd heard his question. And then, to his absolute horror, tears welled up in her eyes and spilled down her cheeks. "Oh, jeez, Addie," he sputtered. "Not again!"

"Sorry." She made an attempt to wipe her face. "And I'm sorry I was such an idiot that night, too. Crying like that—like this—it's, well, so embarrassing. I'm sorry, I really am."

"Here." He got up and grabbed the roll of paper towels by the sink and handed them to her. "Well, this time you're not crying because we're both naked and I'm on top of you, so what is it?"

She shook her head. "Nothing. And please don't use the word 'naked' again. It was just that you asked me 'what's the problem' as if you were going to help me solve it." With that, tears filled her eyes again, but she blinked them back and sniffed. "In case you're wondering, it's been a long time since anyone—okay, a *man*—offered to help like he meant it."

Why would someone offer to help if he didn't mean it? Cal knew he was in way over his head. He sat down again and figured he'd just wait this one out. Then he changed his mind and went into his room to find a clean handkerchief, which he handed to Addie before sitting down again.

"Thank you," she said. Her nose was bright red and her eyes were puffy, but he longed to take her in his arms and hold her. If she were his, he'd haul her onto his lap and let her cry all she wanted on his shoulder. Then he'd solve all the problems in her world, damn it. No matter how serious or silly or incomprehensible they were.

"You want to know about cows," he prompted.

She took a deep breath and seemed to compose herself. "I've been going through my father's papers and I can't make any sense out of them. He stipulated in his will that you were to be paid your salary for the next six months. Does that mean you're going to stay here?"

Cal hesitated. He'd fallen half in love with her that night at Billy's. He could fall the rest of the way in six months, considering that body and those blue eyes, and the sweet way she had of looking at a man as if he was the only person she saw. "I guess," he said, "that's up to you. I mean, if you want a cattle operation or not."

"Do they make money?"

"It depends. Ed—your father—cut back on that, too, these past few years. We used to hire extra men in the summer, but right now it's a small operation. John's pretty much retired now, except for the horses, and you'd have to decide if you want to be a rancher or not."

"You tell me," she said, pushing the books and the calculator across the table toward him. "See what you think of all these accounts, if I can make money at this."

"All right. You mind if I run these figures past John?"

"Of course not." She stood and tossed the used paper towel in the wastebasket next to the fridge. "Thanks for the tea."

"Anytime." He stood, too, but she didn't move toward the door.

"I'll wash this." She tucked the handkerchief in the pocket of her shorts. "Could you just tell me if you're planning on leaving the ranch or not? I mean, I'd like to have some idea, in case I need to look for help, in case I keep the cows."

"I'll stay as long as you need me," he promised, knowing it was the truth. Knowing he was in serious trouble when it came to this particular woman.

"Fair enough." She hesitated again and looked up at him. "Thank you." That tempting little mouth was so close, he could reach her in one stride if he actually lost his mind and decided to try.

"Addie, hon, stop looking at me like that."

"Like what?"

"Like you're waiting to get kissed good-bye," he said, watching her blush. "Don't make me kiss you, because you don't have the time for me to do it right."

She actually laughed, and then said, "You're right," before she turned and walked out the door.

And then it was Cal's turn to be surprised.

"ANY OTHER PROBLEMS besides morning sickness, Mrs. Larson?"

"You mean, besides a craving for spaghetti sauce and basil?"

The young doctor laughed. "I can't do anything about that, except to confirm that you are pregnant, as you knew already. I'll prescribe vitamins, give you the list of do's and don't's and recommend that you find an obstetrician."

"Thank you." Finding a doctor in Nowhere had been simple, as Dr. Records was the only one in town. She would make arrangements to transfer the children's medical records to his office now that she'd met him. "The doctor who delivered the twins is in Austin, but I'm not sure I want to drive seventy miles when I'm in labor."

"I wouldn't recommend it." He scribbled on his prescription pad. "Most women around here use Connie Hoffman, an ob-gyn just south of here, not too far from Round Rock. Forty miles tops."

"Thank you."

"See her soon, all right? This baby is due November sixth, according to my calculations."

"That seems so far away." But she wasn't complaining. She needed all the time she could get.

"And welcome to Nowhere, Mrs. Larson. The town's been waiting to meet you."

"They have?" She tucked the papers he gave her into her bag.

"Sure. Everyone wants to know what you're going to do with that big house. I guess it used to be something, in its day. A few of the old-timers remember what it looked like, and said it was real grand. You don't know it, but you're the talk of the diner right now."

Addie smiled. If they only knew. "I'll have an open house when I'm finished working on it," she promised.

"*After* the baby's born," the doctor cautioned. "You're a widow with five-year-old twins, and you need to conserve your energy. Do you have help? You're going to need to get enough rest these next months."

"I have help," she assured him. "My mother's going to come up on weekends."

His smile was kind. "I see from your chart, your husband died three years ago. Is the baby's father involved in this pregnancy?"

"No." She slung her purse over her shoulder and slipped on her sandals. "Not yet."

Later on, while driving the boys home from their exciting afternoon at their new school, Addie munched on crackers and told herself that everything would work out just fine. But why, when asked about this baby's father, had she added *not yet*? Cal McDonald seemed like a good man, but surely he didn't have to know anything about this baby.

Not yet, anyway.

"HAVE YOU EVER DONE ANY thinkin' 'bout getting married, Calvin?"

"What is this, Ask Cal Questions Day?"

"Huh?" John lifted his baseball cap and scratched his balding head.

"Never mind. The answer to your question is, no, I haven't." Not really. Not since eleventh grade, after having sex with Mary Devlin and thinking that married people got to do that all the time. And in a bed, not in the back of a Buick sedan.

The old man's gaze turned to the main house. Addie's car was there, so she was back from town with the kids. "Not even now?"

"No."

"You might want to reconsider," the old man drawled, turning back to Cal. His grin almost split his face in half. "You've got some real potential here on the Triple J."

"John, don't—"

"Don't give me that, Cal. I seen the way you look at her, and it's not her cookin' you're thinking about, either. Marriage ain't so bad."

"You're an expert?" He smiled and handed the old man a can of soda. "Here. You don't have to drink it here. You're welcome to take it home with you."

John ignored the comment. He sat down in the chair vacated by Addie earlier, and opened his drink. He didn't so much as glance at the pile of notebooks two inches away from his elbow. "I was married once."

"You were?" Somehow Cal couldn't picture it. He'd worked with this man, side by side, for almost twenty years, and he'd never known much about John's personal life. "When?"

"Oh, a long time ago. I admit, I wasn't real good at it."

"What happened? If you don't mind my asking." He sat at the table and stretched his legs out in front of him. John would take his time telling the story, of course.

"Naw, I don't mind. I was sure in love, and she was a sweet girl," he said. "I met her at a dance and we hit it off just fine. Got married 'bout a year later. Got a little ranch near San Marcos, but there was no pleasing her. She got a little strange and then up and left one day." He snapped his fingers. "Just like that, she was gone. I used to wonder what I did wrong—I wondered for years—but things have a way of working out. I've learned that much."

"What does that mean, 'things have a way of working out'?"

Old John shrugged. "They just do. I'm not gonna go into details here, son. I'm just trying to tell you that getting married might do you some good. And our Miss Addie here could sure as hell use a good man by her side."

"That's some story." Cal shook his head. "You

tell me about your unhappy marriage and then you tell me I ought to think about it myself. Does that make any sense?"

"Of course not." The old man looked offended. "There's nothing about falling in love that makes any sense, Cal. That's what I'm trying to tell you!"

"Well, damn it, you won't get any argument from me."

John grinned. "You ever been in love?"

"Sure."

"Ha!"

"You don't believe me?"

"Hell, no! Unless you wuz just a kid when it happened." He took a long swallow from the soda can. "No, when you fall, you're gonna fall hard. And something tells me that I'm going to be around to watch it."

"Don't hold your breath, old man." But Cal's gaze went to the window above the table where, above the tree line, he could see the second story of the main house. John was right, but a man had his pride.

Even if that was all he *did* have.

"IT'S LIKE THAT TELEVISION show, *Queer Eye for the Straight Guy,* only just the opposite," Addie told Kate. She had the portable phone outside so she could talk in private.

"Honey, have you been drinking rum and Cokes again?" Kate laughed. "Or maybe the paint fumes are getting to you."

"Very funny. No, you should see this." She lowered her voice to a whisper. "There are five painters and they're all gorgeous. And possibly straight."

"Possibly?"

"It's not like I can ask. They started yesterday and they're really fast, so if you want to see them, you'll have to come up this week. But you have to promise you won't distract them too much. I really want to get these rooms done."

"I thought you were busy with a plumber."

"He's next week, I hope. He keeps calling and rescheduling, so I don't know. Calls himself the 'Yellow Hose of Texas.'"

"You're making that up."

"I swear, it's painted on his truck. A bright yellow hose with water gushing from one end. Very phallic."

"Speaking of phallic," Kate said, when she had stopped laughing. "How's your ranch hand?"

7

By Thursday Cal had seen all he'd wanted to of the house painters. They'd arrived early on Monday, and piled out of their vans as if they were the answers to a woman's prayers. And since then, Addie had been in that house with them.

Handsome and young, the men had strutted around in white shorts and tank tops spattered with paint. Their music, sometimes salsa, sometimes classical, wafted from the open windows of the big house. And Addie hadn't left the place since they'd arrived. Her friend Kate came one afternoon, though. John reported seeing her car.

Cal thought Addie would have stopped by his place again. He'd bought margarita mix and tequila, fancy instant tea mix and fresh lemons. He went over Ed's notebooks until his eyesight blurred, and he kept his place even cleaner than he usually did, just in case she knocked on the door and wanted to ask about cows.

But she didn't come by, and he blamed the

painters for her absence. She was preoccupied with singing strangers, men who might take advantage of a widow lady with a fat checkbook. So by lunchtime on Thursday, Cal couldn't help but wander over to the big house. Let those fancy painters see that a man was looking out for Mrs. Larson. He gathered up Ed's books and his own notes and, in clean clothes, headed over to check things out for himself. It was his duty, he told himself. He was the manager around here.

"Addie?" He knocked on the kitchen door, but doubted she could hear him. There was music playing somewhere, and the painters were still here, their vans parked next to Addie's wagon on the east side of the house. He opened the screen door and called to her again. "Addie? It's Cal."

He stopped once he'd entered. The room looked different, with fresh, cream paint and fancy red-and-white curtains. The big table was still there, but a vase of flowers sat in its center and fancy, red placemats covered some of its scarred surface, which was now polished and smelling like lemons. After setting the account books at the end of the table, Cal crossed the room and peered into the living area, once Ed's cluttered den, and realized that this, too, was freshly painted and clean.

"Addie? You home?"

"We arrrh all uppa heayh!" It was a man's

voice. Cal heard laughter above the music—some kind of opera, he figured—and he rounded the corner to the foyer and headed up the stairs. He hesitated at the top.

"Addie?"

"Inna heayh!" This time the male voice was followed by Addie's laughter. He turned into her bedroom and saw her up on a ladder, her waist being held by the large, hairy hands of a grinning painter.

"Ah," the man said. "You hava more company inna your bedroom, Adelaide."

Cal frowned. *Adelaide* perched on the top of that ladder and held a long piece of green-flowered fabric as she looked down at him.

"Hi, Cal. I'm trying to decide on curtains."

"Maybe you'd better come down," he said. "Let the painter there hold the stuff while you look."

"I was trying to match the color," she said. "To see if it was really a mint green, or had more sea foam undertones."

"Mint," the black-haired painter said, his hands still on her waist and dropping perilously close to her hips. "Absolutely mint, my darling."

Cal glared at him and the man's eyebrows rose. "You like the color?" he asked Cal.

"Yeah, it's fine." *My darling, my ass.* "Get down, Addie. You're making me nervous."

"I'm fine," she told him, but she did move her

legs and started the descent. The painter released
her waist, and Cal stationed himself at the bottom
of the ladder. He set his own hands on her waist
and guided her, but he didn't step back when she
turned to face him. Instead, he wrapped his arms
around her and hugged her, giving her a brief kiss
on the cheek.

"Let's see, sweetheart," he drawled, as if they
were alone together in her bedroom every day.
"What color have you picked for us now?"

"Cal—" Her eyes narrowed. "What are you—"

"I'm sorry I'm late," he interrupted. "It won't
happen again. Show me the curtains and let the
men get back to work. I'm sure they want to finish after being here all week."

"They finished ten minutes ago. They're packing up now."

"Good." Cal knew damn well what one of them
was doing, and that was coming on to Addie. He
bet the guy used that ladder move on all the
women he painted for. He eyed the guy again, but
the man just winked at him and called something
in another language to the rest of the workers.
"Where are they from?"

"New York. They're Italian. They got tired of
the cold weather up north and moved the whole
business here," she explained. "Didn't they do a
wonderful job?"

He kept his hands on her shoulders. "Took them long enough."

"It's a big house." She looked up at him and began to laugh, so he lifted her by the waist and swung her around gently, removing her from the ladder and the watching painters. She went pale right before his eyes. He watched the color drain out of her face, and she blinked twice and clung to his shoulders.

"Addie?"

"Put me down." Which he did, on the bed.

"Señora?" The largest painter approached the bed, and the other one hovered nearby.

"I'm fine," she assured them, but she dropped her head between her knees while Cal crouched at her feet.

"I'll take care of her." Cal nodded toward the men and they got the message: leave quickly and quietly and let me take care of my woman. The music stopped, and for a few minutes Cal heard the noise of the men gathering their equipment and carrying it downstairs and out the front door. "Addie? What's the matter?"

"I guess I'm not good at heights." Her voice shook slightly, enough so he knew that she was still not feeling well.

"What do you want me to do?"

"Nothing. It'll pass in a few minutes."

"This happens a lot?"

"Sometimes." She took a deep breath, but didn't lift her head. Cal put his hands on her knees and waited for her to explain. "It's a, uh, female thing."

"Okay, so what can I do?" *Female things* were out of his area of expertise, all right.

"How about a cold washcloth?"

"Coming up." He hurried to the bathroom and found stacks of towels on a stand by the sink. The room smelled like fresh paint, an odor that probably had something to do with Addie's dizzy spell. But she'd looked pale at other times, too, which worried him. He wouldn't have thought of her as being delicate, but maybe keeping up with the twins was harder than he thought. John had told him they went to kindergarten in town now, for a few hours a day, which must help. They would be there now, he realized, or he would have seen them.

He ran cold water over the cloth, squeezed the extra water out and returned to the bed. She looked up and smiled at him.

"Don't look so worried," she said. "I'm better now."

"The paint smell couldn't help." He gave her the washcloth and she put it over her forehead and eyes. "I'm going to open some more windows."

"Okay."

"Don't move, all right?"

"I have to get the boys at two-thirty."

"At school?" She nodded. "I'll get them. Can you lie down now?"

"Good idea." Her smile was wobbly, but when she lifted the cloth from her face, he saw that some color had returned to her cheeks. "What do you think of the house? Didn't they do a great job?"

"Yeah," he admitted, but when he thought of that laughing Italian's hands on Addie, he wasn't inclined to give compliments. "But I'm glad they're gone."

"Me, too," she said, leaning back against the pillows. She sighed with contentment. "The rooms are beautiful, but it's been such a *noisy* week."

"Get some rest," Cal said, longing to smooth the hair away from her face. But he stood beside the bed and kept his hands to himself. "I'll get the boys. The school's on Cedar Street, behind the Dairy Queen, right?"

"Yes. Thank you."

"Put the cloth back on your head." It was awkward, standing here looking down at Addie, who smiled as if he'd said something funny. "What?"

"Don't make me kiss you," she replied, laughing up at him. And then the laughter stilled, as she seemed to realize what she had said.

"Making fun of me again?" But he bent over and kissed her anyway. And what began as a brief gesture turned into all the words he couldn't say. *I want you. I miss you. I wish I could hold you.*

"Not really." She reached up and wrapped her arms around his neck. He braced his arms on the side of her head and sat on the edge of the mattress, in the space made by the curve of her waist. And the kiss continued, hot and needy, with the surprising familiarity of kissing Addie when she lay on a bed.

"You were acting all jealous and silly," she murmured against his mouth. "Mario was only being nice."

"He had his hands all over you." Cal's own hands smoothed Addie's hair from her face and repositioned the washcloth.

"What are you doing, Cal?"

"Taking care of you."

"That's not what I meant."

"I know." He brushed his mouth against hers, this time as briefly as he could manage. She'd gone pale again, and when she opened her eyes to gaze up at him, he saw that she looked frightened. Of what? Him? "Addie," he tried, hoping he sounded like he knew what he was talking about. "It'll be okay."

"I know. I'm fine," she whispered. "I don't like heights. Or the smell of paint."

"Yeah," he said. "You just stay still for a while and get some rest." He knew she was just trying to convince herself that she wasn't letting herself be kissed. That she wasn't enjoying it. What *he* was doing, of course, though she might not want to see it, was falling in love with her. Making himself part of her life. Taking care of her.

Cal left the bed, the room and the house. He found the keys to the station wagon hanging on the back porch and he drove to town to get those boys. Addie Larson might not want to admit it, but she needed a man in her life.

In her bed and out of it, the man she needed was him.

And he figured she knew it, too. When Addie wasn't pretending otherwise.

IT HAPPENED AGAIN, of course. Addie knew it would, because she remembered how it was when she'd been pregnant before. The queasy feelings began to settle toward the afternoon, although the dizziness still came at odd, unpredictable times. She needed to be careful that she didn't spend too much time outside in the heat. And she'd arranged to have central air-conditioning installed Monday, so she'd have to make do with the ceiling fans for a few more days. The two air conditioners in the kitchen and the living room managed to keep the downstairs comfortable enough for cooking and eating, though she wondered how her father had survived in the heat of Texas summers.

She gathered up the stack of account books and the pages of Cal's meticulously written notes— not that she could decipher much of his handwriting—and prepared to set out to find her number one ranch hand. She'd take the boys with her, two little whirlwinds designed to discourage intimate conversations between adults and guarantee any business discussions would be kept brief and to the point.

Unfortunately, the heat got to her before she got to Cal.

"Mommy?" Ian peered into her face as she sat down in the dust under a spindly tree. "You okay?"

"Sure. Let's just sit here a minute." Matt plopped beside her and began to draw a road in the dirt, but Ian looked disappointed. He'd wanted to see Cal and maybe get another ride in the truck.

"What about Mr. Cal?"

"He's around somewhere. We'll find him." She closed her eyes, which immediately became a bad idea. So she opened them and focused on her fidgety son, and hoped she wouldn't faint. This was getting ridiculous. She didn't remember being this delicate with the twins. She'd been more like a tank that time, big as a house and mowing down anything in her path. Here she was, not even three months pregnant and unable to take ten steps without swooning. According to the doctor's calculations, she'd start feeling better in the second week of May, when her second trimester began. It couldn't start soon enough.

Though it would come with its own set of problems, like an expanding stomach that would horrify those around her.

Addie forced herself to breathe through her mouth, but the black spots in her vision wouldn't recede. "Ian, honey, do you see Mr. Cal anywhere?"

"Nope." He kicked a dried chunk of horse dung. "Mr. John's in the barn. He waved to me when he went in, and I waved back. Can I go see 'im?"

The barn. A place filled with more dangerous things than a medieval torture chamber, and ten times more appealing to small boys. Addie swallowed and knew she didn't have any choice. If she fainted out here, the boys might not go directly to John, and then who knows what awful things could happen? Beads of sweat broke out on her forehead.

"Ian, I want you to go get Mr. John for me, please." She grabbed his pant leg before he could run off. "Wait. Listen to me very carefully. Don't go near the horses. Go right to Mr. John and call his name when you get to the barn so he knows you're coming." *So he doesn't run over you with a tractor,* she wanted to add. "Tell him your mom needs a little help."

"Me, too?" Poor Matt looked so hopeful, Addie hated to refuse him, but she didn't want both of them running off. They distracted each other.

"No, sweetheart. I need you to stay here in case I need you to find Mr. Cal," she fibbed. She wasn't going to let her other small son go running off alone in the opposite direction, but the child's face lit up at the thought of seeking out the ranch hand. The boys adored him. The fact that he had picked them up at kindergarten yesterday had been the highlight of their lives, according to the excitement at the dinner table that night. Addie had flushed with guilt, not realizing that fathers picked up children from kindergarten and that little boys noticed such things.

"He drives with one hand," Matt announced. "He put gas in your car. We got ice cream."

"I know. You told me." She watched Ian trot toward the barn, his new sneakers kicking up clouds of brown dust as he swerved around cow manure. He held a metal truck in his hand and he waved at the barn door with the other, so he had seen John, thank goodness. No piece of heavy equipment or snorting four-legged animal burst from the dark opening before her small son disappeared inside, so Addie was free to close her eyes. "Come sit with me," she told Matt. "Hold my hand."

"That's a baby thing," the boy grumbled, but he did as he was told.

"But it makes me feel better," she said, which was nothing if not true.

And the next thing she knew, strong arms lifted her from the ground and she was tucked against a strong chest. Cal's chest.

"Addie," she heard, a rumble against her ear. "We're going to get you to the hospital. Hang on."

"I don't need the hospital," she protested, feeling silly and yet very content to be snuggled against Cal's body. The spots were already receding now that her feet were higher than her head and some blood was rushing into her brain.

"It's the heat, Miss Addie. You're just not used to wanderin' around in this kinda sun." John replaced her light wicker hat with his own Stetson. "We're gonna get you in the house and turn up the AC and get you a nice cold drink." He took the boys' hands. "Come on, fellas, let's go."

What she got was Cal McDonald guarding her bed for the rest of the day.

TOUCH OF THE FLU, CRACKERS, *bad back, fainting.* She could see the wheels turning in her mother's head as Paula stared at her from across the table. Addie dropped her gaze and studied the chicken on her plate as if it was a piece of art.

"Really?" Paula drawled. "Mommy fainted today?"

"Yep." Ian, who would certainly grow up to be a television reporter, continued ratting on his mother. "She got all funny looking, and Mr. John called Mr. Cal."

"She just got a little too much sun," John declared. "She needs a better hat. I told her, you need a better hat, gal, one that keeps the sun off your head."

"Yeah," Matt said. "That's what he said. A better hat."

Addie reached for her iced tea. "I'm sure that in this heat I should be drinking more liquids." To prove that she meant what she said, she took a large swallow of iced tea.

"And then," Ian announced, determined to continue on with his little news scoop, "Mr. Cal had to take Mom to bed."

Addie choked and reached for her napkin. She didn't dare look at Cal, who had the ability to look amazingly innocent when he wanted to.

"Well, that was nice of him," Paula told her grandson. "*Very* nice, Mr. Cal. I'm sure Addie appreciated the help."

"Yes, ma'am," he said. "She wasn't doing too well."

"And how are you feeling now, Adelaide?"

Adelaide. Mom was highly aggravated, so Addie chose her words carefully. "Much better, thank you."

"She took a nap," her budding Dan Rather informed everyone.

"A *very* long nap," Matt added. "Mr. John took us for a ride in his truck and we counted the calves all afternoon. Until we got hungry, and then we went to Mr. Cal's house and had peanut butter crackers and ice cream."

No wonder they weren't hungry for supper. Peanut butter and ice cream didn't sound too bad at all.

"And what about you, Mr. Cal?" her mother continued. "Did you count cows, too?"

"He stayed here," Ian explained, puffed up with the weight of all his knowledge. Addie realized she'd given birth to traitors. "In case Mom needed anything."

"Now, now. Cal couldn't leave her alone," John added, his gaze darting from Paula to Addie and back again. "Not feeling well and all."

"No, of course not," her mother said, piercing a piece of potato salad with her fork. "Maybe you should see a doctor, Adelaide."

Cal spoke for the first time in a while. "Maybe that's a good idea. You sure didn't look too healthy this afternoon. You're working too hard, I think."

"Yes," she said. "That must be it. I've been too busy working on the house. What do you think of the new curtains, Mom?"

"Very nice," her mother said, glancing toward the yards of red toile that decorated the long windows and French doors on the wall behind the table. The added wing gave an appearance of a courtyard out those north windows, and Addie had plans to landscape it in the summer. It would be a perfect spot for the children to play. A perfect spot for a baby to sleep in his or her carriage.

Her carriage, Addie hoped.

"Addie?"

She blinked and tried to figure out who had just spoken to her. "Yes?"

Cal cleared his throat. "Have you had a chance to look over the accounts yet? There's an auction on Monday where I might be able to pick up some more calves."

"Sure." She nodded as if she remembered what he was talking about. Every time she tried to read about live stock prices and profits and losses in Cal's scrawling handwriting, she became so sleepy she thought she'd fall over at the desk.

"You haven't read my recommendations," Cal declared. "I thought you wanted to learn all about cows?" She could tell from the slight curve of his lips that he wasn't upset. Her mother stared at her.

"Why would you want to learn about cows?" she asked.

"Because I own a ranch."

"Two weeks ago you were talking about turning this place into a bed-and-breakfast, now you're Barbara Stanwyck?"

"Who's that?"

John shook his head. "Aw, missy, she was a big movie star. Then she went on TV and had a ranch and a mess of sons and all sorts of trouble."

"She wore *great* clothes," Paula added. "She had a tiny waist, and could wear jodhpurs and riding skirts and still look beautiful. I wonder how old she was when that show was on."

"Is she still alive?" John picked up the bowl of potato salad and helped himself to another spoonful. "Miss Addie, you must be feeling better if you can cook like this."

"Thank you. Do you want some more chicken?" She picked up the platter of oven-fried breasts and passed it to her mother. "Mom?"

"Oh, I think Barbara Stanwyck is dead," Paula murmured, giving her daughter an assessing look. A look that could pierce through lead. "But she had a lot of children to help run that ranch of hers, at least on television."

Addie kept her expression carefully blank. "Who would like more coleslaw?"

"That show's still on," John informed them. "All those old shows are still on TV, on the satellite dish. Your dad was sure fond of that dish of his. Claimed it was the best invention known to man."

"Too bad he used a remote control more than a telephone," Paula muttered.

"Some men aren't good communicators, Miss Paula," the old man declared. "Ed had his faults, all right, I won't disagree. But he didn't have no easy time of it growin' up, so I guess some things just didn't get learnt."

"I guess they didn't," Addie's mother agreed, as she helped Matt cut up his chicken. "He wasn't much of a talker."

"No, ma'am."

"That might run in the family, don't you think, Addie?"

She smiled. Or at least she attempted to stretch her lips over her teeth and look happy. "You don't seem to have any trouble holding up your end of the conversation, Mom."

"That's not exactly what I meant, sweetheart."

Addie dared a glance toward Cal. The man looked perfectly calm, despite being busy rescuing Ian from spilling his milk into his dinner plate. The man had the reflexes of a cat. He hadn't minded when she'd spilled her drink on him that night at Billy's. Maybe in those places he'd grown up there'd been a lot of messes, a lot of little scared kids knocking over things.

He would have helped them. It was second nature to him, she saw, to reach over and open a jar of jam or cut up a piece of chicken or move a glass of milk away from the edge of the table.

He was skilled in other ways, too, with those hands of his. She hadn't forgotten yesterday, the way he'd smoothed her hair or held her face when he'd kissed her. Or today, when he'd carried her to the house and held her in his lap in front of the air-conditioning because he was afraid that she would fall off a chair if he let her sit there by herself.

She'd been on her own for so long, she'd forgotten what it was like to have someone worry about her. Other than her mother, which was, of course, totally different. She dared a glance toward Paula, who was eyeing her as if she suspected Addie had spent the afternoon in the middle of a cowboy orgy.

8

PAULA WAITED UNTIL SHE had kissed her darling grandsons and tucked them into bed before cornering her daughter downstairs for a private conversation. Ah, yes. She could smell guilt a mile away. Addie was nothing if not guilty, all right. She sat in that brand-new, maroon leather chair in Ed's freshly painted den and looked as sweet as candy.

Paula sat on the matching couch and moved several *Lord of the Rings* action figures over to a side table before she looked at her daughter again. "Well, Addie? What do you have to say for yourself?"

"About what?"

"You know what." She watched the stubborn chin lift, and the lips tighten. Well, it didn't matter. Addie could get herself in a snit, but it was about time they had a talk. All this fainting business had to stop.

"Just because Cal McDonald was in my bedroom this afternoon doesn't mean we were doing anything wrong. Not that it is any of your business if we were." It was said gently, from a woman who sounded tired. From a woman who had something to hide?

"I don't care if you were entertaining the Dallas Cowboys, my darling, as long as your sons were out of the house when you were doing it," Paula fibbed. She hadn't raised her daughter to behave in a wanton manner, and she didn't think that Addie would cavort with a cowboy she barely knew if she wasn't seriously attracted to him. Addie had never been the boy-crazy type, not even in her teens. "Your sex life is your own concern, I suppose, as long as it didn't end up on the front page of a newspaper somewhere, but—"

"Why would my sex life be in a news—"

"Never mind." Paula held up a hand. "I didn't mean to get off on a tangent. Do whatever you want with Cal, I guess. In your bedroom or in your barn." She stopped to sigh. Maybe it wasn't right to set such an example for the boys, but she could understand Addie's attraction to the handsome rancher. And the man clearly adored her daughter. The way he looked at her would melt steel.

"Mom? I don't want to talk about Cal, and it's been a long day, so I'm going to bed and—"

"Not so fast there, missy," Paula said, not about to be denied. "I'm talking about your health, not your sex life. Dizzy spells? Throwing up in Mr.

Anders's flower pot? Car sickness? Eating crackers? What does all this remind you of?"

"The flu?"

"The flu, my ass." She eyed her daughter, who gulped and didn't say another word. The silence said enough, though, and it was all Paula needed to hear. "I've been running dates in my head for the past couple of hours," she said. "This must have happened some time last winter."

"February," Addie said, looking as white as the window trim.

"That night you went out with Kate?"

"Yes."

"Good heavens, were you *drunk*?" She remembered Addie's unwillingness to discuss her evening the next morning. She'd looked pale and tired, as if she'd been crying and she hadn't slept. Going out with Kate hadn't been much fun, Paula had assumed. Men weren't what they used to be, and the few good ones weren't hanging out at Billy's bar on Valentine's Day.

"A little. But that wasn't why it happened."

Paula leaned back against the plump cushions and closed her eyes. Well, at least Addie wasn't dying of stomach cancer or suffering from some horrible illness. She was pregnant, and the world would go on spinning. Paula took a deep breath and opened her eyes. "All right, then. Who was he?"

"I'd rather not go into the details."

"The name of the baby's father isn't exactly a *detail*," Paula pointed out. "More like a vital piece of information."

"He was just a man in a bar. I didn't know his name."

Paula sighed. It was worse than she had thought, then. She sat quietly for a moment while she thought about the whole mess. "I can't believe you didn't protect yourself. With all the diseases going around, never mind getting pregnant, for heaven's sake, Addie——"

"I'm not a total idiot. We used a condom, but the only thing I can think of is that it was defective." Addie groaned. "I can't believe I'm having this conversation with my mother."

"You're not the only one who can't believe this. When is this little bundle of joy due?"

"Mother, please."

Paula sighed. "I'm sorry. It's going to take me a little time to get used to this."

"You and me both." They sat in silence for a long moment before Addie answered the question. "November sixth."

"You've been to a doctor, then."

"In Nowhere. And I have an appointment with a new gynecologist next month."

"And in the meantime? You're okay?"

"Just suffering from the usual morning sickness, though this is tougher than the last time." She made a face and caressed her flat abdomen. "Maybe this one's a girl, Mom. It already feels different."

"That would be nice," Paula admitted, allowing herself a small smile. But there wasn't much to smile about. Addie already had her hands full, with this big house and two active boys. "Thank goodness you have money now. You have a roof over your head and some security."

"And I have you." Addie grinned at her.

"But a mother is a poor substitute for a husband," Paula felt it necessary to point out. "So I suggest you start figuring out how to get one."

A HUSBAND WAS THE LAST thing Addie wanted. But love? Well, she would like to be loved again. But she didn't think that was going to happen, maybe not until the children were grown up and their mother had time to take a shower without worrying about whether they were getting into trouble.

Long after she'd escaped from the den and her mother's worried expression, Addie lay in her oversize bed and contemplated the mess she was in. She would be showing in another month or so, something she could disguise with baggy shirts and elastic-waist blue jeans. But now that Paula knew, there was no one to hide the news from except the baby's father, and he was sure to question the pregnancy and his role in it. He had a right to, of course. There was no getting around it, no matter how much easier it would be to wish that he would get into his truck and drive off to Montana or Mexico, or anywhere far from here.

She would have to tell him. She would have to make it perfectly clear that she wanted nothing from him. She needed no child support or legal settlements, and she certainly didn't expect him to raise a child that was an accident between strangers. Surely he would have been married by now if he'd been inclined to settle down.

She imagined her attitude would come as a relief, she decided, quickly quashing any thoughts of custody agreements or anything messy. Now that she'd gotten to know him, she didn't think Cal would deliberately cause problems. He was more the kind of man who helped a woman get *out* of trouble, and she was afraid she liked him too much. Otherwise she could fire him, write a check for a year's salary and wave goodbye. He'd never know about the child.

But she couldn't do that. Not now. He had a right to know.

And she would tell him. Eventually. But she had to stop kissing him, first. Had to resist that physical attraction that pulled them together whenever they were in the same room.

And she already knew what kind of trouble that caused. She needed to keep her legs together and her clothes on whenever Cal McDonald was around. She wasn't going to fall for a self-proclaimed hermit and confirmed bachelor. No way.

"Seems to me," John drawled, "if anyone was asking, I'd say that things just couldn't get any better."

"And how do you figure that?" Cal released the calf and watched it race across the corral to its bawling mother.

"Well, there's a real pretty woman in that ranch house now," the old man pointed out. "Seems like a young man might be interested."

"Yeah?" He coiled the rope and slung it over his shoulder. He'd had enough of doctoring animals for one day, but this year's calves looked damn good. That bull he'd talked Ed into buying had turned out to be a good investment.

"She needs a man to help her out around here," John continued, opening the gate for Cal. "You're single and she's single. Seems natural to me."

"She wants to turn this place into a bed-and-breakfast," Cal pointed out. "Some kind of showplace. I don't think that includes cows, not from the way she's talking about profits and losses and old Ed's methods of ranching. And if it doesn't include raising cattle, then I'm out of here."

"You could talk her out of it."

"It's not my place to talk her into, or out of, anything." Cal headed back to the barn, John following close behind. "It's different for you," he told the old man. "You've got your place for life, and you've got a pension. I've got six months— four, now—and then I can leave. She can fire me anytime she wants—"

"But she won't," the old man declared. "I can't handle this place by myself."

"If she gets rid of the cattle, you can. You can keep a few of the best horses for the kids, and hire a teenager to help you with the heavy stuff on weekends. You'd be fine."

"And where would you be?"

"I have some money saved," he said. "I can probably figure out how to get a small place. Or I can get a job on another ranch, just like you said."

The old man swore. "This ain't right," he grumbled. "You and Miss Addie are two healthy, young folks who could make a damn fine couple."

"She's out of my league."

"No way. Why don't you give that little gal a break and take her out to eat somewhere nice? She's been working herself half to death on that house, and she's fed us some damn fine meals, too. Hell, I'd be glad to take her out myself."

Cal grinned. "Well, you should go right ahead, John. Just ask her."

"I think she'd rather go out with you. But I'll take care of the boys," the old man declared. "That'll be my contribution."

"I'm not interested," he lied. "She's the kind of woman who wants a ring on her finger and a husband in her bed."

"Well, of course she does!" John turned red and started to huff. "She's a respectable young woman. And you'd make a damn fine husband, Cal. No matter what you say. She looks at you like you make the sun rise, you know."

He didn't know.

"And," John continued, "those little boys worship the ground you walk on. And you can't tell me that you don't like her, cuz I've seen you watching her, too. And you carried her up to her bedroom and took care of her when she was sick."

"Anyone would do that." Cal put away the medical supplies and checked on the horses, with John still following in the dimly lit barn.

"Maybe. At least take her out somewhere nice and see how she's feeling."

"All right," Cal conceded, knowing that the old man wouldn't quit until he heard the answer he wanted: Cal would take Addie out to dinner. But maybe it *was* time he left here, before things got any more complicated. He liked Addie a hell of a lot more than he wanted to admit. There had been something about her that night at Billy's, something that made him come out of his shell and carry the woman to bed. He'd wanted to make love to her and dance with her and protect her with his life.

Now here she was, living right here with him, and all he wanted to do was run away.

"I THOUGHT WE COULD GO OUT," Cal repeated Sunday afternoon, watching Addie wash the lunch dishes at the kitchen sink. "To dinner."

"When?"

"Tonight." He figured the timing was right. Mrs. Johanson had spent the weekend, as she did every weekend. But she'd driven out of the driveway twenty minutes ago, right on schedule at half past one on Sunday afternoon, and John was standing by to babysit the boys. He'd take her out to a nice meal, show her that he could be more than a bad memory in a motel. And then he'd give her his resignation.

"Well," he prompted, wishing she'd turn away from scrubbing that metal pan. "What do you say?"

"I don't have much of an appetite these days."

"Just order soup." She rinsed the pot and set it in the drainer. He noticed that her hands were shaking.

"I might get dizzy."

"It's air-conditioned."

"But—"

"Then I'll carry you to the car and drive you home." He leaned closer and looked into her face. Her cheeks were pink enough, and she didn't look the least bit sick. "Your mother told John you were going to see a doctor."

"Yes. Just to stop her from worrying. I might need to eat a little better."

"You can start tonight."

She smiled and tossed the dishcloth at him. "Okay. What time do you want to go out? And how fancy is this place?"

"We can leave at six, John's going to watch the boys and wear anything you want." He turned to hurry out of the kitchen before she changed her mind. This had been easier than he'd imagined.

"Hey, Cal?"

Damn. He turned. "What?"

"Did my mother put you up to this?"

Now that was a question he hadn't expected. But from the look in her pretty blue eyes, he guessed Addie was serious. "What's your mother got to do with us going out tonight?"

"She wants me to get married." Her smile just about dropped him to his knees. And so did the word "marriage."

"I was just thinking about a couple of steaks and maybe dessert, sweetheart."

"Well, all right." She started to laugh. "But I wouldn't put it past my mother to start matchmaking."

"I'm the last person she'd toss your way," Cal declared, tipping his hat before he reached for the door once again. "See you later." He got out of there as fast as he could, before Addie could change her mind and decide that her mother wouldn't approve. Paula Johanson frightened him. She was pleasant enough, always polite and well-mannered, but Cal was always afraid he was going to do something wrong when she was around. Like spill his coffee or knock over a chair. If Paula had ever walked in when he was spread out on a bed with her daughter, there would have been hell to pay.

He wasn't thinking of hell five hours later when he saw Addie. No, she looked like an angel, in a floaty white skirt and a damn fine top that hugged every inch of her and matched her eyes. Her hair was loose and curly, and her mouth—well, he didn't need to stare at her mouth. He took her hand and tugged her toward the door.

"You look beautiful," was about all he could manage without embarrassing himself.

"You don't look too bad yourself," she said,

smiling up at him as they went down the side steps to the driveway. He'd worn a copper silk tweed sports jacket he'd bought in Austin last year for a friend's wedding, but he'd decided a tie was too formal with the white shirt. Now he wasn't so sure.

"Thanks. I'm glad we're getting off the ranch."

"Me, too." She sounded as if she meant it, which pleased him. But the boys danced around the newly washed truck and asked John why they couldn't go along.

"Because John would be lonesome," their mother told them, which seemed to do the trick. Cal ushered her into the passenger seat and shut the door before the boys could cause a scene and give the old man a hard time. Old John took both of the boys by the hands and looked as if he knew exactly what he was doing.

"We'll be back in about three hours," Cal promised him. "I owe you one."

"You owe me more'n that," the old man drawled, winking. "Like maybe a nice, new slow cooker or something."

"You be good," Addie said, rolling down the window to give one last order. "Eight o'clock bedtime, no matter what. Earlier if you're naughty."

"Dam— Darn right," John agreed. "Now wave yer mom good-bye and go back to yer supper."

"Thanks, John."

He tipped his hat, and Cal started up the truck and turned it around to head down the drive. "That wasn't too hard," he said, once they'd made it a hundred yards away from the house.

"Poor John. I'm feeling guilty already."

"You have the cell phone?"

"Yes."

"We can be back here in twenty minutes if he needs us," Cal promised.

"Why are you doing this?"

Damn. A trick question. There was no way to answer this one without getting in trouble, and here they hadn't even had appetizers yet. "Doing what?" he stalled. He turned on the radio and hoped a little Faith Hill would help.

"Taking me out."

"John's idea. He's matchmaking." That seemed to surprise her, because Addie didn't say any more for at least a mile or two. He looked over to see her gazing at him with those big eyes of hers. He'd give a million dollars to know what she was thinking.

"We sure started out the wrong way."

"I'm sorry about that." *Sort of*, he amended, remembering the feel of her body underneath his. It was hard to be sorry about having great sex with a beautiful woman.

"Yes," she said. "So am I. When I saw you that day at the ranch, I couldn't believe my bad luck."

"Thanks." He smiled at her to show he knew she was kidding.

She reached over and touched his shoulder. "I didn't mean it like that, Cal. I just never expected that my awful mistake was going to show up in my backyard. I don't go around having sex with strangers in motels after drinking in bars."

"I didn't think you did." He almost drove off the road. What the hell had he been thinking? She was a widow with kids, a pretty woman who no doubt wanted another husband. Anyone could tell she needed a man around, especially since she seemed so damn fragile. But he was about as far away from husband material as, well, John.

"It's not something I intend to do again," she said, after a long moment of silence.

"I went to Billy's the next Saturday looking for you," Cal said.

"I gave up rum and Cokes. And nights out with Kate." She shuddered. "I don't know what got into me that night."

"Neither one of us was thinking straight," he pointed out, but Cal knew he hadn't been the same since he'd taken her on that bed. He'd wondered how to get in touch with her. He'd worried about the broken condom. And he'd driven to Billy's on Saturday nights for four weeks in a row, hoping to see her or her dark-haired girlfriend, so he could get her name. He'd wanted to see her again, wanted to make love to her for hours and wipe away the tears he hoped she wouldn't shed.

"No," she said. "That's true. In fact, there's something—" She stopped.

"What?"

"Nothing." He noticed she was gripping her hands together and her knuckles were white. "I guess you like living in Nowhere. Have you ever thought of living anywhere else?"

"I've thought of getting my own place," he admitted. This was his opening. He could tell her that he was leaving after the summer was over, or sooner if he could find someone to help John.

"In Texas?"

"I imagine."

"I see."

Cal glanced sideways and saw that she'd gone pale. "Addie? You okay?"

"I'm fine. So do you have any family around here?"

"Not that I know of, not anymore. I guess John's the closest thing to family that I have." He smiled. "He thinks you need a husband."

"He's probably been talking to my mother. That's all she thinks about."

"And you don't?"

"No."

She sounded sure of herself, Cal realized. Which, he told himself, was a relief.

"THE WOMAN AT THE BAR—the one in the dark-green dress—keeps staring at you." Addie sipped her minted iced tea and watched Cal shift uncomfortably in his chair. He didn't so much as glance over his shoulder. "Old girlfriend, maybe?"

"Maybe."

"She's quite beautiful. A redhead. About thirty-five, I'd guess, but it's hard to tell in the dim light."

"I imagine that's Deb Stornaway," Cal replied. "She works in real estate around here and runs a small ranch north of town."

"Oh." Addie didn't like the piercing jealousy that landed in the pit of her stomach. How ridiculous. Cal was a handsome man who had spent most of his life in Nowhere. Of course he would know a lot of women. Addie looked down at her strawberry shortcake, a dessert that was larger than Cal's Stetson, and picked up her fork.

There hadn't been a good time to discuss having a baby, Addie realized. Not over dinner, when Cal had shared stories about her father with her. He'd referred to his own family twice, to explain that he barely remembered a mother who ran off and a father who pretty much left his young son to fend for himself until the social workers came to take him away.

"We dated for a while," Cal explained. "About three years ago."

"What happened?"

"She wanted something permanent," he said, pushing his half-eaten apple pie aside.

"And you didn't."

"No."

"Why not?"

He smiled. "Maybe I'm getting too old, too set in my ways. Like John."

"You're not so old."

"Almost forty."

"Yes, I know. You have a birthday coming up."

He stared at her. "John again?"

"No. I've been going through my father's papers," she explained. "Your birthday is May twenty-first."

"That's right." He took a sip of his coffee and set the mug down. "There was something I wanted to talk to you about tonight."

"I wanted to talk to you, too," she heard herself say. "I've put it off for a while now but it's only fair that you know what's going on." She took a deep breath.

"You're ending the cattle operation," he said, his eyes dark and unreadable.

"Well, no—"

"No?"

"There was an article in the paper about a ranch near us that's raising some special breed of beef cattle." She wished she could remember the name of the darn things. "Saint something."

"Santa Gertrudis?"

"That's it. Are they very expensive?"

"They are." He leaned back in his chair. "Sweetheart, I thought you wanted a bed-and-breakfast operation, not a cattle ranch."

"Eventually," she said. "But I need to keep money coming in so the ranch is self-sufficient."

"Like its owner," Cal said.

"Yes." She finished the rest of her dessert while he discussed the merits of a new breeding program. *There would be other times to talk to him,* she promised herself. And maybe she needed to do it somewhere private, without an ex-girlfriend watching or a waitress interrupting to refill his coffee.

There was time, Addie told herself. *Neither one of them were going anywhere.*

9

"I LET THE LITTLE FELLAS watch TV after they put their pj's on," John whispered. "And they fell asleep so I just left them here."

"That's okay. I'll get them to bed." Addie smiled. Matt lay sprawled on the couch while Ian was asleep on the floor, his head nestled against an oversize pillow. "I'll take them upstairs. Thank you for taking such good care of them."

"No problem, Miss Addie," the old man drawled. "They're fine boys. Didn't give me no trouble at all, except for falling asleep before I could get them upstairs in their beds."

"I'm glad they behaved themselves." She had given them strict instructions to obey John and to go to sleep when they were told to, but she suspected John was too softhearted to be strict with them. "They were pretty excited about you being here."

"Did you two have a good time?" The old man grinned. "It's sure nice when two young people can go out and be alone together."

"We had a lovely dinner," Addie assured him, but Cal frowned. John stifled a laugh and moved toward the door. "I'll be heading home now, though. I'm feeling a bit sleepy myself. Good night, Miss Addie. 'Night, Cal."

"Good night," she said, before leaning over Matt to wake him.

"Don't bother the boy," Cal said, stepping closer. "I'll carry him upstairs for you."

"All right." She followed him up the kitchen staircase and turned on a small, corner lamp so Cal could see. "It's this one," she said, pulling back the covers on her son's bed. Cal deposited the sleeping child onto the mattress and Addie covered Matt with the striped sheet.

They did the same with Ian, who grumbled in his sleep and opened his eyes once to stare blankly at the rancher holding him. "Mr. Cal?"

"Go to sleep, boy," Cal whispered. "You're in your own bed now."

Ian blinked twice before closing his eyes and rolling over on his side. "Okay," he mumbled before falling asleep.

"Thanks," Addie whispered, once the boys were settled in their beds. Cal started for the stairs, but Addie stopped him. "Wait," she whispered. "I have that article up here, the one about the fancy cattle and how that ranch is making money selling beef that doesn't have additives or chemicals."

She hurried past her bathroom and closets, through the narrow passageway that connected her room to the children's, to find the magazine for Cal to read. She heard his footsteps behind her as she knelt down and rifled through the stack of reading material next to her bed. She wasn't surprised to see the man standing there, looking at her in the dim light that came from the bathroom's night-light.

"I found it," she said, coming to her feet. "There's an auction every June and—"

"Addie." He reached out to take her hand. "Forget the cattle for a minute."

"But—" His hand was warm, the skin rough around her fingers.

"I'm going to kiss you good-night now," Cal said. "I'm done talking about cows."

"Are you sure?" She couldn't help smiling up at him in the darkness. "This magazine article has a lot of information you might want—"

"I'm sure," he said. Cal took the magazine and tossed it onto the bed, then tugged her closer so that their bodies touched. Her breasts were against his body, and she had the overwhelming desire to rip off his shirt and bury her face in his naked chest. She remembered it being a very impressive part of him. "No more ranch talk, sweetheart. I'm going to take advantage of being in your bedroom for a few minutes."

Oh, good, she wanted to say. Even though she had no business kissing the man, or starting something that she shouldn't really finish. But she was only human, she told herself, gazing up at the man who held her so gently. "And how are you going to do that?"

He brought his mouth down to hers, brushed her cheek with his lips. "Well, I thought I'd kiss you for a while," he whispered. "Maybe a few hours."

"Hours?"

"Mmm." His lips moved across hers. "Unlike our first date."

"Please don't remind me." The immediate physical reaction to his kisses was all too familiar. She told herself she was lonely. She reminded herself that her hormones were raging out of control. She forgave herself for kicking off her sandals and pulling him closer.

"It's one of my fondest memories," he murmured against her mouth. "Up until the end, when you ran out of the motel room."

She wasn't running now, she realized. That wide expanse of king-size bed was only inches away, but Addie knew she had to resist hauling the cowboy onto the mattress. She was a respectable woman, a mother, a landowner and a woman of reason and good sense. But he kissed her again, not so gently this time. And the respectable woman of good sense looped her arms around his neck and pulled him even closer.

"We shouldn't," she managed to say, once he'd lifted his mouth. Her body tingled in all the right places and reminded her that she was courting trouble.

"Yeah," he said. "I know."

"Although I suppose it's not that terrible, since we've done it before—"

"That one time doesn't count," the man growled. "Not really."

Oh, it counted, she wanted to say. Enough to make a baby, despite the circumstances.

"I have to lock the doors," she managed to whisper into his chest.

"I did." His fingers lifted her blouse and caressed her bare skin. For one instant of panic, she wondered if he could tell that her body was rounder. But she told herself that there was no way he could remember the shape of her waist or the curve of her abdomen, not from the brief time they'd spent naked together.

"How can we do this?" she whispered. "We *know* each other now."

His hands swept along her back and unhooked her bra. His soft chuckle tickled her neck. "You only have sex with strangers, Addie?"

"Of course not, but—" Oh, dear. Those wonderful hands of his unbuttoned the front of her blouse. He swept it off her shoulders and down her arms before tossing it to the floor. Then he did the same to her bra, releasing her breasts so that her sensitive nipples brushed against his starched cotton shirt.

"Addie?"

She'd closed her eyes and leaned against him as his hands stroked her bare back, then lower, to unzip her skirt and ease it past her hips to the floor. "Mmm?"

"You're beautiful, just as I remembered."

"It was dark," she countered, embarrassed by the compliment as she stood there wearing nothing but pale-blue bikini underpants.

"Not that dark."

No, not that dark. And not that long ago, either. But this time they knew each other. This time they were friends, or something more than acquaintances. And this time they were in a house—her house—and weren't exactly alone. His large hands caressed her breasts, weighed their heaviness, moved lower to her waist. His fingers skimmed the satin cloth that covered the last bit of skin. He made short work of removing her underwear, surprising her by lowering himself on his haunches and working the scrap of fabric down her legs. She held his shoulders and lifted one foot and then the other, kicking the underwear aside with an abandon she didn't recognize in herself. His lips touched her stomach and his hands held her hips still.

"Cal," she breathed, wondering how much longer she could stand up as his lips trailed kisses lower. His warm breath moved over her like hot silk, stroking and teasing the sensitive flesh exposed to his lips. It was like every erotic novel she'd ever read, but this was real. He rested his head on her abdomen and took a deep breath before he spoke.

"Come to bed, Addie."

"Yes."

He lifted her easily and deposited her on the bed. She pushed the covers aside and slid beneath the sheets while Cal undressed.

"This is crazy," she managed to say as he tossed his shirt to the floor. "We're going to regret this in the morning."

"Why?" He sat down on the bed and tugged off his boots before he turned to smile at her. "It's going to last longer than ten minutes this time. And hopefully neither one of us is going to run off into the night."

She thought about running. But she was naked, and didn't want to be anyplace but in bed with Cal McDonald, who was taking too long to remove his jeans. She wanted him, plain and simple. Her breasts ached to be touched, her body hummed with unspent passion, and when Cal, now blessedly naked and impressively aroused, slipped into bed beside her, Addie shivered.

"What's wrong?" He leaned over her and brushed a lock of hair from her forehead. "Are you cold?"

"No." He urged her closer, and she went into his arms as easily as if she did so every night. It was like coming home after a long, hard trip, an erotic reunion of two people who might not have realized how much they missed each other.

She'd missed him, though. She'd known that every night she'd lain alone in her bed and remembered how he felt deep inside of her. His body slid against hers as he kissed her, his tongue teasing hers as their bodies entwined underneath the cotton sheet. His deep, low sound of pleasure echoed her own need, and she wanted him inside of her again, wanted to feel him as part of her. He moved her onto her back and took his time caressing her body and kissing a path downward, to the vee between her legs, then gently pushed her thighs apart to allow him entrance.

Addie bit back a cry as his mouth found her. Her body, so newly pregnant and sensitive, reacted quickly to the touch of his lips, and she flinched at the startling pleasure that his mouth gave her. His long fingers slid across her wetness, slipped inside, opened her for him. She tried not to climax right then and there, but her body was on fire and there was no stopping the spiraling orgasm that Cal coaxed so easily from her. She closed her eyes and gasped as the climax burst from her, whirling from the very core of her being and turning her breathless and shaking.

He didn't leave her for a long moment. His mouth absorbed the aftershocks of her orgasm while his fingers moved in and out with slow, soothing motions. She eventually caught her breath and wondered how on earth this man could have this kind of effect on her.

He eased away from the bed, retrieved the condom he had left on the nightstand and returned to her. She reached for him before he could cover himself; she wanted to feel him, needed to run her fingertips along the hard length of him and learn how he liked to be touched.

Cal groaned, but when she would have taken him in her hand and pleasured him with her mouth, he gently removed her hand and lifted it away from his body.

"It feels too good, sweetheart," was all he said, his voice raspy with passion as he slid the condom on. "Not that I don't appreciate the gesture, but keep that up and I'll embarrass myself and have to go home early."

"We wouldn't want that." She smiled into his eyes before he leaned forward and kissed her. And she was lost once again as Cal moved over her and urged her thighs apart. She was ready for him, of course. He'd made sure of that. And they fit together as perfectly as she remembered, though tonight she could appreciate it for more than simply sating lust, filling a lonely need to be loved, if only for a little while.

Tonight was so much different, so much better.

Tonight she knew his name. She called it a long time later when she climaxed, moments before he plunged deep and hard, finding his own release inside of her.

He pulled the covers over them, settled her into his arms. She was asleep almost immediately, but not before thinking that she might have made another big mistake. Not by making love to Cal, she realized, snuggling into his wide chest, but by falling in love with him.

"Hi."

Cal opened his eyes and saw the twins' faces inches away from his own. They looked at him as if they were happy to see him this morning, which was unsettling to a man who had made love to their mother twice last night and could have done so again this morning if he'd been left alone to seduce the woman curled so contentedly against him.

"Hi," he whispered, knowing Addie was still asleep. Her face was tucked against his back; he could feel the length of that beautiful body pressed against him. Thank God they were both covered with the sheet, or the kids would really have something to tell their grandmother next weekend.

"What are you doin' here?" Ian asked, looking over at his mother as if he couldn't believe that she was sleeping so late.

"Sleeping," was the only thing Cal could think to say. He knew he'd locked the doors, but the boys must have gone downstairs and come up the front staircase. Cal hadn't thought of locking the door that led to the hall. Next time he'd be more careful.

"Oh. Mommy's sleeping?"

"She sure is. Don't wake her up, all right? She's really tired." The boys frowned.

"We're hungry," Matt said. "And we hafta go to school."

Cal peered at the clock on the nightstand. "It's only five-thirty. I think you have plenty of time." They didn't look convinced. "Go downstairs and watch TV or something, and I'll be down in a minute."

"Really?" Ian's face brightened and he turned to Matt. "See? I told you."

"Told him what?" Cal asked, but Matt only grinned before the boys turned and hurried out of the room. He heard them laughing as they hurried down the main staircase, and hoped the sound wouldn't wake Addie.

"Oh, no," she groaned. *Too late*, Cal realized. He turned to watch her make a frantic attempt to sit up. She was tousled and lovely, caught in a tangle of sheets and cursing quietly under her breath.

"Addie, it's okay. They didn't see anything." He put his hand on her arm but she shook it off.

"They saw you in my bed. What on earth are they going to think?"

"That you were sleeping. They're only five."

"Going on six. Old enough to remember they saw their mother in bed with a man. A naked man." She managed to get out of the bed, a sheet draped modestly around her body, and hurried across the room to close and lock the door. "I knew it was a mistake."

"What was?"

"This. Us. You." She stopped at the foot of the bed and gazed at him. "Definitely a mistake."

Cal shook his head. "Come here."

"I can't. I have to make breakfast and act like a mother."

He sat up and held out his hand. "Come here, Addie. Say good morning."

She stood where she was, but she returned his smile. "Good morning, Cal."

"Good morning, Addie. Did you sleep well?"

"Yes. When I had a chance." She walked around the bed and took his offered hand. He tugged her closer and kissed her lightly on the lips before releasing her.

"Go back to bed," he said. "I'll go down and feed the boys."

"No." Addie moved away. "I'll do it. Just go, okay?"

"All right." He told himself it was for the best. He had no reason to act like he belonged here, even in the early hours of a Monday morning.

Cal had lain awake for a long time while Addie had slept curled against him. He hadn't planned on this. Hadn't dared to hope that dinner would turn into lovemaking, that a simple evening out would end with this sweet and willing woman welcoming him into her bed.

He was truly amazed. And yet he'd known for weeks, since he'd learned she was a widow, that they would end up together again. There was too much passion between them, too much awareness of each other to ignore. They'd come together whether they'd planned to or not.

But passion was all it could be. Nothing more. He'd been alone too long to think of anything else.

10

"So now what?"

"I don't know." Addie held the cell phone to her ear as she sat outside in the car, waiting for the boys to come out of school. She was early, but she'd needed a reason to leave the ranch and avoid running into Cal. Every time she thought of making love to him last night, she turned red and dropped something. She'd already broken her favorite coffee mug and one of her new cereal bowls. Tonight she was serving dinner on paper plates. "I'm not sure how to act."

"Well, you called an expert," Kate drawled. "Your cowboy took you out to dinner, took you to bed and took you to, um, heights of ecstasy, right?"

"Yes." She blushed, remembering some of the more erotic details.

"And in the morning you sent him back to his little hut and morphed back into Supermom."

"The boys woke up and came into the bedroom.

What else could I have done?" When she'd rushed downstairs to the kitchen, they were already arguing over what kind of cereal to pour into their bowls. They'd looked disappointed to see her and not their hero, but Addie had told them that Cal had to go take care of the cows.

"Have you seen him today?"

"No."

"Have you tried to see him?"

"Of course not." She picked up the cup of iced tea she'd bought from the Dairy Queen. "Kate, there's more to this, something else you don't know."

"Uh-oh. Just a minute. I'm going to close my office door." There were footsteps, Kate told someone to take a message, and there was laughter and then the sound of a door closing. "Okay. Tell me now."

"I'm pregnant." There was silence. Such a long stretch of silence that Addie finally prompted, "Kate? Are you still there?"

"I'm here. I was just thinking that I wish I hadn't quit smoking."

"It happened that night at Billy's, on Valentine's Day. The condom broke," she explained. "I couldn't believe it, either. Not until I started having morning sickness."

"Good heavens, Addie, you're a regular baby-making factory. You need to get married, and fast. What does Cowboy Cal have to say about all of this?"

"That's the hard part," Addie said, taking another sip of iced tea. "He doesn't know it. He's going to think it's a trap, that I'm looking for a husband and a father for my kids—all three of them."

"Can you blame him?" Kate sighed. "Fertile Myrtle arrives on the ranch and presents him with a baby. I don't think he's going to jump for joy."

"That makes two of us not jumping," Addie said. "And you should have heard my mother's reaction."

"Paula knows? You're a brave woman."

"She figured it out."

"I hate to remind you, Addie, but Cal's going to notice eventually, too. When is the baby due?"

"Early November. I have time."

"Time for what?"

"Time to tell him, I guess."

"And then what? Get married? Ride off into the sunset together?"

"No, of course not." Addie sighed as the doors opened and the children were led outside into the sunshine. "I don't expect that. I'm perfectly able to raise this child by myself. And it's not like I'm in some kind of relationship with Cal McDonald. He's practically a stranger."

"It may not be a typical romance, but you're in

love with him," Kate declared. "Otherwise you wouldn't sound so miserable."

"I have to go," Addie said. "The boys are coming. And of course I'm not in love with him."

Kate laughed. "Yeah, right. You wouldn't have slept with him again if you weren't feeling something. I know you."

"But—"

"Dinner tonight," her friend declared. "I'll be at your place by seven and I'll bring pizza. You can eat pizza, can't you?"

"Sure. But—"

"We'll talk then," Kate promised. "In the meantime, try to be nice to your cowboy."

With that piece of advice, the phone clicked off and Addie tossed her cell phone into her purse. Even if she was falling in love with Cal McDonald, it didn't mean anything. They were two people thrust into an awkward situation, even if only one of them realized it.

"SHE HAS COMPANY," JOHN informed him. "Just in case you were thinking about going over to see her."

Cal reached for the rag hanging by the shop door and attempted to wipe the grease off his hands. Ed's old tractor wasn't going to last much longer, but Cal was determined to get another season out of the old beast. "You have anything else to do around here except watch what's going on at the big house?"

The old man chuckled. "No. Those horses aren't much work, not for an old pro like me. I'm giving the boys riding lessons tomorrow, though. I could use your help, if you're gonna be around."

"Sure." He tossed the rag aside and looked toward the house. "Who's there now? The plumber again?"

"Nah. The guy installing the air-conditioning system's still here, and then Kate drove up. Maybe we should walk over there and see if the ladies need anything."

"Like what?" He needed a shower and a beer, nothing more. Just because he'd made love to Addie for half the night didn't mean he had to start following her around. She'd made it clear this morning that she didn't want him around when the boys could ask questions. He wondered how she'd explained him sleeping over last night.

John shrugged. "I dunno. Maybe they'd just like some male company."

"If Addie wants us, she knows how to find us." He'd be damned if he'd walk into that house looking for her.

"You're in a mood."

Cal shook his head. "Sorry. I'm heading home to clean up, and I'm staying there."

"What'd you two talk about last night? You have a good time?"

"She's been reading about Santa Gertrudis," he told the old man, whose eyebrows rose. "Wants to raise chemical-free beef."

"Guess she's not going to sell the cattle, then." John's grin threatened to split his face apart. "Guess she's going to keep you around. Aren't you happy you took my advice and asked the little gal out?"

"Yeah," Cal told him. "Sure." He hoped the old man never found out what he and Addie had done for the rest of the night. He didn't doubt John would come after him with a shotgun if he knew that Cal hadn't left Addie's bed until after dawn.

He wanted nothing more than to see her again, to walk into that kitchen and put his arms around her and carry her upstairs to bed. He wanted to make sure she was feeling all right, wanted to watch her sleep. Wanted to make love to her again and wake up next to her.

Later, in the brutal emptiness of his small house, Cal wondered if he had been better off before Addie moved here, when he hadn't known what he had been missing.

SHE COULD TAKE THE MAGAZINE to him. She could discuss the upcoming auction and pretend she cared about raising beef cattle. She could stroll past the barns—they were her barns, after all—and inquire about the livestock.

Or, as Kate suggested with great hilarity, she could put on her sexiest nightgown and invite Cal to the house for a nightcap. Call him, her friend had said. And she was tempted, of course. They had some things to discuss, but she wanted to have all of her clothes on when she talked to him about the baby.

She would make it clear that he wasn't to feel obligated, that she could manage quite well on her own. The last thing she needed, as she'd explained to her incredulous friend, was a man who felt forced to be with her.

"You're crazy," Kate had said. "He's a good man—or seems to be—and you're going to have three fatherless kids. If I were in your shoes, I'd admit I was falling for the guy and do whatever it took to keep him in my life."

"It's not that easy," she'd countered, wondering if it possibly could be.

"You're making things more complicated than they need to be," Kate had insisted. But then again, she'd had a few rum and Cokes with her pizza, and decided to spend the night and go into work late the next morning. "Take the man to bed, Addie. *Keep* the man in bed. If he's not in love with you now, he soon will be. After all, he's been on this ranch for twenty years. How grim is that? And how lucky is he to have you move in?"

Addie had been only too happy to say good-night and avoid any more advice. She'd waited three more days—and spent three more sleepless nights—before she decided what to do about the cowboy. She put on baggy shorts, a loose T-shirt and a wide-brimmed hat, and headed outside to see if he was around. His truck was parked near his house and she found him behind the largest barn, doctoring calves. The little guys were bawling their heads off and their mothers, on the other side of the fence, weren't happy about the separation, either.

Cal looked up at her and waved. She walked up to the fence and perched on the top rung. They would be friends, she decided. And then, once that had been established, she would decide when to tell him the rest.

"Hey," he said, walking toward her. He wiped his brow with his sleeve and tipped his Stetson back to reveal a sweat-soaked forehead. "What are you doing out here?"

"Looking for you." He actually took her breath away, something Addie didn't like admitting to herself. Good-looking and coated with dust, the man had that competent strength about him that made her want to jump into his arms.

"Yeah?" He grinned. "I thought you were avoiding me."

"I was," she admitted. "A little."

"You didn't have to." He took off his gloves and put one hand on her bare knee, sending shivers up her leg. "I wasn't about to come walking into your bedroom."

"I know." Though each night she'd wondered what she would have done if he'd appeared in the doorway. She didn't think she'd have kicked him out.

"Not that I didn't think about it," he admitted, smiling up at her. "You're a hard woman to forget."

"Thank you."

"You're welcome." They smiled at each other for a long moment. Addie took a deep breath and tried to remember why she was out here. "How's everything up at the house? Did the boys ask a lot of questions?"

She flushed. "I told them that you spent the night because I was afraid of thunderstorms."

"And are you?" His warm hand slid above her knee, his long fingers disappearing under the hem of her khaki shorts.

"Well, yes. A little." She was more afraid she was going to fall backwards off the fence if his hand slid any higher up her thigh.

"Have you ever been made love to on a pile of hay?"

"Not lately, no."

"Ever?"

"No." She wriggled. "Stop that."

"I can promise you it won't take long." He smiled and lifted her off the fence. "Unless you want it to last all afternoon."

"We can't do this," she muttered, but he was leading her toward the barn, and she followed willingly. "What about John?"

"Went to town to pick up supplies. And the boys?"

"In school. I pick them up at two-thirty." She saw him look at his watch, and then he smiled.

"That gives us an hour and a half. Plenty of time."

"You lied," she murmured later from a lovely position in the hayloft. She was sprawled on top of Cal's naked body. He lay on an old horse blanket on a pile of hay, his hands caressing her bottom and keeping her from wriggling away. Sunlight filtered from the cracks in the barn boards, and the heat was intense. Addie decided she could blame her increasing dizziness on sexual satisfaction.

"About what?"

"We *didn't* have plenty of time. I have to hurry up and get to town now."

"Too much kissing," he said. "Next time we're going to skip all the foreplay and go right to the good stuff."

"Okay. I like the good stuff." She laughed and knew she was definitely in trouble. In love and in trouble. Anyone would tell her this was the perfect situation, to be in love with the man who'd fathered her child. But if he wasn't in love with her?

She gazed down at him. He was still inside of her, though she could rectify that easily enough. He looked sexy and content, satisfied and pleased with himself and the way he'd spent a hot Friday afternoon. But he wasn't in love with her. She knew better than to delude herself into thinking this was more than pure lust.

"What?" He frowned. "What's wrong?"

"Nothing. I have to go."

"Want to go dancing tonight? Billy's is sure to have a band."

"Can't." She slipped off him and fell onto the blanket where her clothes lay in a pile. "The boys are having a new friend spend the night. We're renting movies."

"Maybe next week."

"Maybe." She dressed quickly, as did Cal. She didn't question why she felt the need to hurry away. She supposed she didn't want him to see that she was falling in love with him. How embarrassing that would be for both of them.

Then Addie realized that she was standing in a hayloft with straw sticking out of her bra.

"SO, YOU TWO WENT OUT TO dinner a few weeks ago." Addie's mother handed him a tall glass of lemonade. "I hope you like vodka."

"Thank you." Cal sat down on one of the new porch rocking chairs and wondered if Addie was going to join them soon. "Where's Addie?"

"Inside putting the finishing touches on dinner. I'm to keep you out of the kitchen until she's ready. She's feeling better now that she has the air-conditioning all through the house. It's a good improvement, don't you think?"

"Yes, ma'am." He hadn't seen much of Addie for the past few weeks. There had been no more hayloft visits, and his offers to go out to dinner had been sweetly rejected. The invitation to dinner tonight had been a welcome surprise, though he'd known it would be a family meal, with John included, too. "I think she's feeling fine."

In fact, Addie had been looking damn good. And he even thought she might be gaining weight.

Paula looked relieved. She leaned forward and lowered her voice. "I've wanted to talk you for a while now. I think it's wonderful that you and my daughter are dating each other."

"Dating," he repeated, wondering if that one dinner out qualified. And Paula thought it was wonderful? That was a shock.

"You know," she said, pausing to take a large swallow of her drink. "People make mistakes."

"Yes, they sure do." Cal decided he needed to be drinking, too. He looked over his shoulder, hoping to see John appear in the yard, but he was alone with Paula and there was no escape in sight.

"Everyone does," the woman continued. "Some are bigger mistakes than others, of course. But things happen between two people, especially when one of those people is lonely and may have had too much to drink."

"I'm afraid that's true," he managed to say. Shit. Paula knew about that night at Billy's. Why in hell had Addie told her mother about it? He would never understand women and their need to tell each other everything they did.

"I love my daughter and I don't want to see her hurt, Cal."

"I would never hurt Addie," he promised, feeling a little desperate to explain himself. "That night at Billy's just happened. We got a little carried away, I'll admit, but that was out of character for both of us." There. He hoped she wouldn't toss

him off the porch, but hell, she was the one who'd
brought it up. She stared at him like she'd never
seen him before. Her mouth opened but no words
came out. "Mrs. Johanson? Paula?"

"*You're* the father? *You?*" She leaned back in
the rocker and blinked. "How on earth did that
happen?"

"I'm the father? The father of what?" What the
hell had the woman put in his drink? Cal frowned.
"What are you talking about?"

"Addie's going to have a baby," she said. "By
some man she met on Valentine's Day. And since
the two of you are dating and you seem like a
good man to have around, I hoped I could pave
the way for you to understand what happened
and maybe, you know, forgive her. Stand by her.
Be here for her." Paula's eyes filled with tears. "I
was trying to explain that my daughter doesn't go
around sleeping with men she meets in bars, so
that when the time came, you'd understand and
wouldn't dump her. And now I find out that *you're*
the man in the bar. I can't believe that you two
knew each other all this time."

The damn condom. He'd suspected that it
broke that night, but he'd been in such a hurry to
go after Addie that he hadn't paid much attention. He'd just been trying to get dressed so that
he wouldn't lose her.

"This is all too much," Paula muttered, draining the rest of her drink. "Addie should have told me."

"Addie should have told *you*?" He laughed, but he wasn't amused. "I think she should have told *me*, don't you?"

"I'm sure she was going to," Paula said, but she didn't sound convinced. "I mean, you were going to notice sooner or later, weren't you?"

"Yeah." He stood and turned to head into the house. "I think it's time your daughter and I talked about this, don't you?"

"Now?" Paula jumped out of her chair and put her hand on his arm. "This might not be the best time to—"

"Mrs. Johanson—"

"Paula," she corrected, looking up at him with a worried expression. "This is all my fault, Cal. I shouldn't have meddled."

"It's between Addie and me now," he said. He was going to be a father. Addie was pregnant. No wonder she'd been feeling poorly. All that time, and she hadn't told him. Why the hell not? Was she intending to tell him, or was she going to let him think the baby belonged to someone else? And what if it did? No. It was his, only his. He'd bet money on it.

"Of course you want to talk to her, but could you wait until after dinner?" She trailed after him as he entered the house and strode into the kitchen. He smelled roast beef and apple pie, heard the laughter of the children and saw red and white balloons hanging from the chandelier over the battered farm table. There was a fancy, red tablecloth and crepe paper streamers, country music blaring from the stereo in the den and Addie, an apron tied around her waist, smiling at him.

"Happy birthday," she said, her beautiful eyes filled with laughter as she noted his stunned expression.

"Happy birthday!" the boys yelled, and John clapped him on the shoulder.

"Sit down," Addie said, motioning him toward the seat at the head of the table. "The boys and I have been planning this all week. Are you surprised?"

Cal forced his frozen lips into a smile. "Yes," he managed to say. "I've never been more surprised in my life."

11

ADDIE BLINKED BACK THE sudden spring of tears.
Obviously Cal had never had a surprise birthday
party before, or he wouldn't have looked so
shocked. The man had actually turned pale as he
stood in her kitchen. She knew he'd grown up in
group homes, but she hadn't expected him to react
this way to a simple birthday. The boys were all
over him, but he didn't seem to notice their excitement except to tousle Ian's hair and pat Matt on
the shoulder. He stood there by the table and
stared down at her as if he'd never seen her before.

"Sit down," she said again. "You're the guest of
honor so you sit here."

He sat, but so slowly she wondered if he was
all right. Come to think of it, he didn't look too
happy about his party. She hoped he wasn't one
of those people who hated birthdays. The boys
bounced around him, chattering about how they'd
helped frost the cake and wrap the presents. John
chuckled and asked how it felt to be forty. And her

mother, who looked a little flustered by all the commotion, refilled Cal's drink.

"Here," Paula said, setting another spiked lemonade on the table. "Drink up. I'll make another pitcher right away."

"We thought you should have a party, especially for your fortieth," Addie said, placing a platter of sliced roast beef on the table. "Come on, everyone. Sit down and eat."

"I wish I could remember when I turned forty." John took a seat next to Paula, with Matthew next to him. "Sure was a long time ago, though. I don't think I had a party. You feel any older, Cal?"

"Yes," he said, giving Addie a strange look. "I sure do."

She put the rest of the food on the table and sat down on Cal's right, Ian beside her. Cal stared at her apron and she hurried to untie the old thing. She'd bought a new mint green sundress for the occasion, something that looked cool and made her appear slim, but she was afraid that she couldn't hide her condition much longer. Next week, she promised herself. She'd gather her courage and tell him next week.

"You look very pretty tonight," Cal said, taking two slices of meat from the platter John offered him.

"Thank you."

"New dress?"

"Yes." She blushed and passed the bowl of whipped potatoes to him. "Gravy?"

"Please."

Cal helped Matthew fix his plate as if he'd been doing it for years, but he didn't smile. He didn't look happy about his party.

"Mom made a pie, too," Ian announced. "In case Mr. Cal doesn't like cake. Do you like cake?"

"Yes," Cal said. "I like it a lot."

Matt grinned. "I said you liked cake. With choc'late frosting."

"Absolutely."

Addie watched him with the boys and her heart lifted. Maybe this could work out somehow. Maybe he would hold her and tell her that he was in love with her, too. That he would move heaven and hell to make her happy.

She was wrong, she discovered later. He led her outside after John and Paula had volunteered to clean up the kitchen and the boys had fought over putting the candles on the cake.

"When were you going to tell me?" Cal stood looking down at her and waited for an answer.

"It was a surprise party, Cal. That was the point."

"About the baby, Addie," he countered. "When were you going to tell me about the baby? Or were you?"

"I was," she replied, her heart racing. Had he noticed the roundness of her belly and figured it out? Oh, Lord. "Of course I was."

He didn't look convinced. "How much longer were you going to let this go on? Until you needed a ride to the hospital?"

She put her hands on the small swell of her abdomen. "I'm barely three months pregnant, Cal. I didn't know what you'd say, and I didn't want you to think I was trying to trap you into marriage or anything."

"Or anything," he repeated, wincing. "You didn't think I deserved to know?"

Addie lifted her chin. "I decided it wasn't going to be your problem."

"*You* decided?" The man looked as if he was going to explode. "You're having my child and you didn't want to involve me?"

"I didn't think—"

"Mom! We got the candles on!" She turned to see Ian poking his head out the door. "We gotta light the candles now!"

"We're coming." She turned back to Cal. "They want to sing 'Happy Birthday' to you. Come on."

"We'll talk later, Addie," he said, his gaze dropping once more to her abdomen as if he couldn't believe there was a baby growing inside.

"Yes," she promised, though she would have

rather scrubbed horse stalls. How she managed to get through the next hours, she didn't know. Cal obligingly blew out his candles and assured the boys he'd made a wish. He opened his presents— a new pair of work gloves from John, the new Johnny Cash CD from Paula—and dutifully admired the new boots she and the boys had picked out for him in town.

"John told us what size," Addie said, hoping Cal wouldn't think she'd been snooping through his house. "And of course you can exchange them."

"They're great," he assured her as the boys hugged him and leaned against his chair. "Thank you."

"Cake," Ian said. "You want ice cream, too?"

Yes, Cal wanted ice cream. Cutting the two-layer chocolate cake, slicing the pie and dishing out ice cream gave Addie a reason to keep busy. Her mother kept looking at her with a worried expression.

"I'm sorry," Paula whispered later, when the men had taken their coffee, and the twins, into the den. "I let the cat out of the bag."

"You told Cal?"

"Well, I didn't know he was the father. I was just talking about how people make mistakes." She set a stack of dirty dishes by the sink. "I was doing a little matchmaking and it backfired."

"No kidding." Sometimes she wished she'd been an orphan. "He's angry about this."

"He'll get over it. This actually couldn't have worked out better," Paula continued, reaching for a sponge. "This thing with you and Cal, well, it's like it was meant to be."

"Not really, Mom. I think you're simplifying things too much. Just because Cal and I have been, um, intimate, doesn't mean that we're automatically meant for each other."

"You could do worse," her mother sniffed. "And sometimes the most simple solutions are the best."

"I'll keep that in mind." But she didn't think any of this was going to be simple. Not from the expression on the rancher's face when he looked at her stomach as if she was incubating an alien from Mars.

"COME OUTSIDE WITH ME."

"Just a sec. I have to put—"

"Now, Addie. Your mother will take care of the boys," Cal said, then raised his voice. "Paula? Addie and I are going to my place for a while."

"Take your time," she called, ensconced on the sofa with both boys snuggled up next to her. "We're watching *Bonanza*."

"*Bonanza?*" Cal gathered up his birthday gifts.

"It's their latest obsession." Addie looked as if

she was going to run, not that he blamed her. He'd heard pregnant women were sensitive, and he could believe it. He'd spent his birthday meal looking at her and remembering the times she'd gotten dizzy, and how he'd seen her eating crackers and looking sick. He should have guessed what was going on. But he hadn't given it much thought. And now he was trying to hold on to to his temper, trying to understand why Addie had preferred to keep her secret instead of tell him the truth. He was going to be a father and it scared the hell out of him.

"Why didn't you tell me? What were you afraid of?" he asked, once they were alone in his house. He turned on one light and stood in the middle of the room, waiting for an answer.

She didn't answer, damn her. She stayed near the door and crossed her arms over her chest. She looked fragile and pale and very, very lovely, but he didn't know what was going on in that head.

"Afraid I wouldn't believe it was mine?"

"No." He walked over to her, lifted her by the waist and deposited her on his narrow bed.

"What are you doing?"

"I can't have a conversation with a woman who looks like she's going to run out the door. *Is* it mine, Addie?"

"Yes."

"And when is it due?"

"Quit saying 'it.' November sixth. The twins came early, though, but twins do that. I had a C-section, so I will—" She stopped, her blue eyes gazing at him. "Look, you have a right to be angry, I guess, but—"

"You *guess?* What are you doing, lady? You slept with a guy you met in a bar."

"The biggest mistake of my life," she said. "But thank you for reminding me. You slept with a woman you met in a bar. And you seemed real familiar with that motel, too, Cal, no matter what you said about putting friends up there when they couldn't drive home."

"Neither one of us was real smart that night."

"No. And you don't have to worry about me. Or the baby."

"I don't." Now that was a laugh. He had done nothing but worry about her since the day he found out she was a widow. He'd done a lot more than worry, too. He'd taken her to bed and he'd taken her to the barn, and he'd figured he'd died and gone to heaven each time. And now he felt like a fool of the biggest kind. "What do you want from me, Addie?"

"Nothing. I'm fine."

"We'll get married," he heard himself say. "Right away."

She went still. "Why?"

"Because that child is going to have my name."

"No."

"No?"

"I'm not looking for a husband," Addie informed him.

"You damn well need one."

"Not necessarily, cowboy." She bounced off the bed and left the house, slamming the door behind her. Cal stood in his empty house once again. He had the sinking feeling that he'd just handled everything the wrong way.

THIS WAS ALL VERY UNFAIR, Addie decided, walking back to the house. He'd reacted to the news much the way she'd expected, though she'd hoped he'd be happier. In her stupid, hopeful heart, she'd wondered if he would take her in his arms and tell her how much she meant to him.

Yeah, right. Like that was going to happen anytime soon.

Addie sat on the porch rather than going inside to face her family. It was a hot night, but there was a pleasant enough breeze. She could sit here for a while and lick her wounds. He wanted to give the baby his name. He wanted marriage.

It's not as if she hadn't thought about it herself. She'd pictured waking up next to him in the morning, having that big, warm body next to her in bed, her boys depending on him for attention and guidance, a baby knowing what it was like to have a father to hold her.

All those things were tempting and lovely to think about, but the reality was that Cal felt trapped and angry and responsible. Not the best requisites for a groom.

And she preferred to be alone, she really did. It was certainly better than marrying a man who was doing it for all the wrong reasons. She could take care of herself. She'd been proving that all along.

Nothing was going to change now.

"HOW'S IT GOING?"

John shook his head, sending Paula's high hopes plummeting. "They're not talking much," he said. "But I can't stop grinning, Paula. Can you imagine? A baby in this old place? Why, it's too good to be true." He grinned even wider. "Why, when Cal told me, I thought I'd fall right over."

"He seems okay with it, then?" She pulled her overnight bag out of her car and shut the door, but there was no sign of Addie or the boys.

"Seems to. Except he can't get Miss Addie to agree to get married and give that baby a name."

Paula sighed. "She's a stubborn girl. I've been hoping she and Cal would talk things over." She'd waited a week to return to the ranch, and then she'd come up on Saturday afternoon, hoping that she could babysit and let the young people have some time to work out their differences.

"Not that I know of. Cal's stomping around here, not saying anything at all, and Miss Addie's in that house all the time. The boys are doing real good with their riding lessons, though. Wait 'til you see them on their ponies. They took to those horses like they'd grown up here."

"I'm glad." She headed toward the house. "Where is everyone?"

"Cal drove off somewhere, and the rest of them are inside where it's nice and cool."

"What are we going to do, John?"

He lifted his hat and scratched his bald head. "Well, Miss Paula, I don't think there's anything we *can* do. But I've known Cal for twenty years now, since he was a skinny young kid cleaning barns, and he's a good man. He'll make this right, I'm sure he will."

"Addie's stubborn," Paula pointed out again, wishing her daughter would bend a little. Being independent was one thing, but being stupid was another. "But I know she likes him. Liking Cal's a good start, I'm sure."

"Seems like we ought to be able to figure out how to help things along," the old cowboy drawled. "Two smart folks like us."

"You have any ideas?"

"We could lock 'em in the tractor shed, see what happens." He chuckled.

"I'd rather lock them in a bedroom," Paula muttered, heading toward the front door. Another passionate encounter might help them think straight. "Whatever happened to the days of shotgun weddings?"

"Gone," John sighed. "But I got a couple of rifles if you want 'em."

"If things don't get settled before November," Paula said, "I'll take you up on that offer."

"How are you?"

Addie looked up from slicing cantaloupe for a fruit salad and saw Cal standing inside the door. He looked tired, but he didn't look angry. She'd missed him. She'd half hoped, half dreaded he'd come to the house, and yet it had been almost two weeks since his birthday. Two weeks since he'd found out she was pregnant.

"Fine. I'm making a salad to take to the kindergarten. They're having a last-day-of-school party tomorrow."

"I heard. It's all they can talk about." He closed the door behind him and walked over to her. "Marriage isn't such a bad idea, you know."

"You're going to tell me you want to be a father?"

"I'm trying to tell you to keep an open mind."

She finished cutting the last slice of melon and covered the bowl with plastic wrap. "You're being very old-fashioned, Cal."

"Old-fashioned," he repeated, sounding slightly amused. "I'm going to take that as a compliment."

She set the bowl in the refrigerator and tried to ignore the fact that he was standing so close. "That's not a bad thing," she said. "I didn't mean it as an insult."

"It's probably old-fashioned to want to carry you upstairs to bed."

Addie stilled. "I don't think making love is going to make things any better."

"No?" He easily lifted her into his arms, as easily as he had that night outside of Billy's. "The boys are asleep and it's just you and me. Maybe we should try it and see."

"Sex isn't going to solve anything, Cal." But she rested her head on his shoulder and relaxed. She was in love with him, for heaven's sake. She wasn't in any condition to resist being carried to bed by the man she'd fallen in love with.

12

WHEN HE WOKE THE NEXT morning, it was to discover Addie still asleep beside him. Her smooth, naked body was tucked against his side, and her breathing was light and even. He'd delighted in the changes in her body, in the small signs of pregnancy he was able to feel when he touched her. He wondered what she'd look like in three months, in five. He couldn't wait to see.

His woman. His child. Somehow, without realizing it, he'd been given the gift of a lifetime, a surprise of such magnitude that he could barely imagine the impact. He'd been alone all his life, except for Ed—a miserly yet fair employer—and John, the kind of grandfather everyone should have, even if he did like to meddle.

Even now he had nothing to offer this woman. Nothing except his name and his protection. Addie owned this place, she had plenty of money and she was smart enough to figure out how to run a cattle ranch, whether he was here or not. But she was pregnant with his child, and that counted for something.

That counted for a hell of a lot.

"Cal?" He turned to see Addie's gaze on his face.

"Good morning."

She smiled, a sleepy, satisfied smile that boded well for this morning's discussion of marriage. "Good morning. What time is it?"

"Not quite six. I thought you'd sleep later."

"I'm an early riser," she murmured, not looking at all as if she was ready to bounce out of bed.

"There's been no sound from the boys, so you can go back to sleep." He turned on his side and moved a lock of hair away from her cheek.

"Maybe I'll just lie here and enjoy the quiet." She smiled and his heart contracted.

"Marry me, Addie," he said softly. "We'll make it work, I promise." She didn't respond for a long moment, but she looked as if she was thinking over the suggestion.

"Why?" she asked finally.

Cal didn't hide his surprise. "That's obvious, isn't it? Because we're going to have a child."

"But there should be more to it than that," Addie said.

"More," he repeated. "What else can I offer, Addie?" He waited for her to answer, but she simply looked at him with those questioning blue eyes.

"I don't want to marry you," she said. "Not like this."

He moved away so she wouldn't see how hurt he was. He didn't know what she wanted from him, but he wasn't going to beg. Cal left the bed and retrieved his clothes. "I don't know what you want, sweetheart. But I wish to hell you'd figure it out soon."

"I want—" She stopped suddenly, obviously unwilling to tell him. Or maybe she didn't know. He'd heard pregnant women could be a little odd at times.

"What?" he prompted, throwing on his clothes. "Tell me and I'll make it happen."

"You can't." Her eyes filled with tears, and something within him snapped. He was tired of being alone, tired of living on the outside looking in. And she expected him to stand by and let it happen with his own child?

"I get it," he snapped. And he was afraid he understood all too well. "Here's the deal, Addie," he said, approaching the bed, while she struggled to sit up and pull the sheet over her full breasts. "You either marry me or I'm out of here."

"That's quite an ultimatum." She looked up at him as if she didn't quite believe he was serious.

"I want you. And I want the baby. I'll take care of your sons and I'll run your ranch. What more do you want?" He suspected she wanted him to fall on his knees and express his undying devotion, but he was no hypocrite. He offered what he could, and no more.

"No," she whispered. "That's not enough."

"Not good enough for you, I guess," he said, trying to smile to show that his heart wasn't smashed.

"That's not it at all," she insisted. "What about love, Cal? We don't—"

"What?" he asked into the silence. "We don't *what*?"

She didn't answer, and he knew that she couldn't say the words.

"Never mind. I can take care of myself," Addie said, looking fragile and determined.

"If that's the way you want it," Cal said, "that's the way you can have it." He took a deep breath and went to the door, but before he opened it he turned back to the woman in the bed. "You have my resignation, sweetheart. I'll be out of here as soon as I've packed."

He didn't wait for her reply. He left the room, and the house, as fast as he could, before he could weaken and change his mind. He'd had years of experience being alone, and he damn well could continue.

But he didn't have much experience with

love, and he wasn't about to say something he didn't mean. But if he could love anyone, it would be Addie.

SHE DIDN'T CRY. SHE HAD what she wanted, didn't she? He was leaving, which she'd hoped for weeks ago. She was better off alone, of course. Better off managing things by herself. She could take care of her children and her life without Cal McDonald.

He didn't love her. He'd said as much before he left. He was honest, and she was foolish. So foolish to fall in love with the man in such a short time. From the second he'd touched her, taken her hand and led her onto the dance floor that night, she'd felt as if she'd found someone she could wrap her arms and heart around. There had been that mind-numbing passion, but she'd felt she could trust him, too. And she still felt that way, even if he had just walked out.

"You have too much pride," Kate told her later over the phone. "Admit you're in love with him and take him any way you can get him. Men like that don't come around very often."

Yes, Addie agreed. Men like Cal were few and far between. But she didn't know how to make him love her. "I'm not going to trap him into marriage," she insisted, feeling righteous and lonely.

"How do you know he doesn't love you, you

idiot? Have you asked him?" Kate's voice had become shrill.

"Of course not. I'm not *that* pathetic."

"It's a damn good question," Kate insisted. "And he might have an interesting answer. I like Cal. If I wasn't dating your air conditioner installer—and by the way, he's absolutely fabulous, in bed and out of it—I'd go after him myself."

"Over my dead body," Addie said, wondering if she'd sent Cal into the arms of the beautiful real estate agent from town. "Besides, he's not your type."

"No, Addie. He's yours. So put on some makeup and go hunt him down. Give him a chance to sweep you off your feet again."

"He's angry."

"He's hurt. Go say you're sorry and haul him back to bed. Or I'm going to call your mother."

"That's not even remotely funny." Addie certainly didn't want to hear what Paula would have to say about Cal leaving the ranch, and his unborn child. She'd be here this afternoon and find out soon enough, though.

The boys ran into the kitchen and started hollering about going to the barn. "I have to go. The boys are going riding before the party at school."

"Good luck," Kate said. "And don't be a fool. Go after him."

Easier said than done.

"BUT THIS ISN'T RIGHT," John sputtered. "Calvin, you know darn well this isn't right at all."

"I offered to marry her," Cal said, shoving his small pile of clothing into a cardboard box. "I begged her to marry me. She said no."

"She'll change her mind," the old man insisted. "Surely she'll come to her senses any day now."

"I can't do it, John." He gathered up an armful of books and tossed them into a paper bag. "I can't stay here and watch from a distance while she raises my child and dates the local plumber, or the guy who owns the insurance business on Main Street. She thinks she's better off without me and maybe she's right."

"Aw, Cal, come on, son." He followed Cal into the kitchen and out the door, but Cal didn't slow down. He was determined to load up his truck and get the hell out of Nowhere.

"Dammit, McDonald," the old man muttered. "You've gone too far."

"Not far enough," Cal said, and went back into his house for another load as John shuffled toward his own place, presumably to cuss in private.

Not long afterwards, Cal caught a glimpse of Addie and her sons heading toward the corral, but that didn't slow Cal's packing. He watched to see if she would head his way after taking the boys to John for their riding lesson, but she returned to the house without looking in his direction. She wore sunglasses, a floppy hat and the green dress she'd worn for his birthday party. She looked pregnant and luscious and completely unattainable.

So he returned to his house, opened a can of soda and continued to pack. He didn't know he had so much stuff, but with any luck he could be out of here in twenty minutes. He'd just put the last box in the back of the truck when he heard John calling him.

"Cal!"

He went around to the front of the truck to see the old man standing there holding a rifle. "What are you doing, John?"

"Making a point," the old man growled. "I don't want no one going nowhere, least of all the father of my next great-grandchild."

"What?" The old man had spent too much time in the sun, was Cal's first thought. The other was that John had suddenly gone insane.

"You heard me." He lifted the rifle to his shoulder and pointed it toward Cal. "Get away from that truck, Cal, and come with me to see Addie. We'll get this settled in no time at all."

"Put the gun down," Cal said, holding up his hands as if he was about to be arrested. "We'll go inside and talk. I still have a couple of Mountain Dews in the fridge and—"

"Nope." He gestured with the rifle, and Cal

couldn't tell if this was some kind of joke or the desperate act of a man who'd watched too many television westerns. "We're going to talk to Addie, and you're getting married."

"John?" Addie came hurrying down the road, kicking up little balls of dust with her green sandals. "What on earth are you doing?"

"Miss Addie, you're just the person I wanted to see." He grinned and lowered the gun as she approached. "Cal here has something he wants to say."

Cal put his arms down and hoped like hell that the gun wasn't loaded.

"John, what's going on?" She eyed the gun as if it was a three-headed snake. "Put that thing away before it hurts someone."

"Not yet," the old man replied. "Soon, though. Right after we sort things out." He glared at Cal. "Well, son? Tell the woman how you feel about her."

"John—"

"Do it," the old man said. "You've never been short on brains, but you're acting like a fool. Do you love my granddaughter or not?"

Cal was saved from having to answer when Addie spoke.

"Your granddaughter?" Addie stared at the old man. "Who's that?"

"You are, darlin'." John grinned. "I wasn't

going to say nothing for a while, cuz I'm not real proud of what kind of father I was, and I sure as heck couldn't go behind Ed's back and see my granddaughter, since Ed figured we wouldn't be welcome and I don't blame him, but heck, it's clear that you need someone looking out for you."

Addie's mouth dropped open. "You're my *grandfather*?"

"Yes, darlin', I sure am. Edward Johanson Senior," he announced. "John's short for Johanson. Always was." He nodded toward Cal. "And I want you to have the best husband in the whole darn world, so that's why Cal here is going to make an honest woman out of you."

Her gaze dropped to the gun and she laughed. "You were going to shoot him for me?"

"Nah, it's not loaded." He grinned. "I just wanted to make sure Cal didn't leave. Not 'til you two worked out your differences."

"He doesn't have to marry me," Addie insisted. "Really he doesn't."

But John was not so easily convinced. "Do you love him, Addie? You do, don't you?"

"Of course," she answered. "But that's not the point."

Cal ignored the rifle and moved toward her. "You love me?"

"You don't have to look so surprised." She turned pink. "I thought it was obvious."

"Tell her you love her," John ordered, and Cal spoke right up.

"I love you, Addie." Surprisingly, he got the words past the lump in his throat.

She didn't look at all convinced, but John was pleased enough to lower the rifle and grin at both of them. "There," he said. "Was that so darn difficult?"

"No," Cal lied. If love meant that the very sight of Addie made his heart pound and his blood race and his breath get stuck in his throat, then he was in love. If leaving her made him feel close to death, then he was in love. If the thought of marrying her caused heaven to open up and shower him with undeserved blessings, then he was in love.

Cal removed the rifle from the old man's hands. He double-checked to make sure it wasn't loaded before he set it inside the truck. "Jeez, John, have you been drinking?"

"I'm glad we're family," Addie told John, and kissed his cheek. "Wait until the boys find out that—" She stopped and pulled away. "John, where are Matt and Ian?"

"I sent them back to the house. Didn't have the heart—or the time—for lessons this morning. They weren't real happy, but I watched 'em 'til they reached the porch—"

"They're not there," she said, turning white.

"But I watched them go home." John looked as if he was going to burst into tears, and Cal frowned. Those two kids could get into a pile of trouble on this place, but they'd only shown interest in one thing so far, and that was riding.

"The horses," Cal said. "Do you think they went riding on their own?"

"Oh, Lord," John groaned. "I'd saddled up the mares before changin' my plans. Do you think—"

"Check your house," Cal told him. "Just in case they went there looking for you."

Addie had already started running toward the barn, so Cal jumped in his truck and drove in the opposite direction, around the bend and up a slope that would give him a good view of the eastern quarter of the property. If those boys were on horses, he stood a good chance of catching sight of the little devils. And a better chance of finding them before they broke their necks.

THE LONGEST TWENTY MINUTES of her life passed before Addie saw the truck approaching from north of the cattle pens. It took a few seconds for her to see the horses tied to its bumper, the reason the truck was moving so slowly, and to realize that Cal had found the boys.

"John!"

"I see, Miss Addie, I see." He sat down on a tree stump and wiped his brow with an old, red handkerchief. "Those boys just about gave me a heart attack. I could be too old for this kind of excitement."

"You were waving a rifle around a little while ago," she pointed out, her heart suddenly as light as the clouds drifting overhead. The boys must be safe, or Cal would be driving faster. She could make out two small heads next to Cal through the window. They were sitting up. Their bodies weren't bruised and broken in a ditch somewhere. They were safe.

"They need a damn good spanking," her grandfather muttered. "They could have hurt those horses."

"Don't worry. They're going to be punished." Starting with missing the party this afternoon. Then there would be no more riding lessons for a long while, plus being confined to their room. Without toys. She didn't believe in spanking, but she was close to making an exception.

"You could do a lot worse than him, you know," John said, watching the truck approach. "He's a good man. He'll do right by you."

"Yes, I know. I guess I wanted more than duty," she confessed. "I love him very much."

"And Cal loves you," the old man declared. "He's just about crazy from loving you. Has been from the start, Addie, since you first came here. Maybe he doesn't say it, but he's shown you every day that he cares for you." He motioned toward the truck, now so close she could see the boys waving to her. "I guess it's up to you to get him to stay."

"Without holding a gun on him," Addie said.

"I'd save that as a last resort." John struggled to his feet as the truck pulled to a stop in front of them. "But if you need some bullets, just let me know."

She didn't need ammunition, but she could have used some courage. Cal hauled two shaking boys from the truck and turned them over to their mother, who grabbed their dirty hands and threatened to keep them in their room until August. John untied the horses and led them away after giving the boys a piece of his mind.

They cried.

Addie hardened her heart and took them to the house, Cal following close behind. She sent them upstairs to wash up and get in their beds for the afternoon, and they cried even harder.

"Hey," Cal said, before they reached the staircase. He crouched down in front of them. "You disobeyed John and you put your horses in danger. Are you going to do that again?"

They shook their heads and sniffed.

"Good. So you learned something. Remember what I said in the truck?" They collapsed into his arms, making Addie wish she could do the same thing. She watched him hug them, then he said something she couldn't hear and sent them upstairs.

Cal stood and turned toward her. "They're going to do a lot worse, you know."

"Yes." She shuddered to think of it. "It's a good thing you were here. You're not really leaving me, are you?" She had seen the boxes in his truck, and knew he was ready to drive off.

"I think," Cal said, moving closer to stand in front of her, "I'm going to have to stick around. Just in case you need me again."

She looped her arms around his neck and gazed into his dark eyes. "I do. Need you."

"Yes." His hands slid down her hips and pulled her body against his. "I know. But you're going to have to marry me eventually, sweetheart. Your grandfather was serious about a shotgun wedding."

"Say it again," she whispered.

"I love you, Adelaide Larson." He smiled before he kissed her.

"Why didn't you say so before?" She'd have given half the ranch to hear those words from him.

"Ah, Addie," he sighed, burying his face in her hair. "Those aren't easy words. And until you came along, I guess I didn't even know what they meant. I guess I had to think about leaving you before I realized I couldn't go."

"Are you proposing again?" She tilted her head and looked up. Her cowboy smiled, and Addie knew that she didn't have to worry any longer.

"Sweetheart, I'm going to keep asking until you say yes. I don't give up easily."

"I like that in a man."

"Say yes," he growled, then picked her up and swung her into his arms. "And we'll start on the honeymoon right away."

"We have about five and a half months," Addie teased.

"There's no need to rush into anything."

"No way," he said. "I don't want to give you time to change your mind."

"A grandfather and a husband all in one week-end? I can't believe my luck." She reached up and caressed his cheek.

"Neither can I," Cal whispered. "Do you think the kids will take a nap?"

"Even if they don't, there are five other bed-rooms in this house," Addie pointed out. "And they all have locks on the doors."

His arms tightened around her as he carried her down the hall toward the empty front bed-room. "This is a heck of a lot better than the Sleepy Time Motel."

"Yes," she whispered into his throat. Had she

been any happier, she would have floated right out of his arms. "And this time we know each other's names."

Epilogue

"SHE'S THE PRETTIEST THING I've ever seen," John declared. He wore his best overalls and a clean, white shirt, his boots polished to perfection and the few hairs on his head combed neatly in place.

Paula tucked her arm in his and wiped her eyes with a tissue from her purse.

"This is the happiest day of my life," she said. "I had my doubts, John, but I think we can stop worrying now. It's going to be all right."

"Well, 'course it is." He patted his daughter-in-law's hand. "These things have a way of working out."

Kate hurried down the corridor, the twins jogging beside her. "Well? Have you seen her yet?"

"See for yourself. She's dressed in pink, of course, and she has dark hair," Paula said, holding out her arms to her grandsons. "Come here, sweethearts, and see your new sister."

"Where's Mom?" Ian asked.

"And where's Dad?" Matt wanted to know.

Since the wedding, the boys had insisted on calling Cal "Dad" every chance they got. John swore they were going to wear out the word, but Paula still blinked back tears when she saw Cal interact with her grandsons. He was a true gentleman, and she'd long forgiven him for carrying her daughter to a motel room two hours after meeting her.

"They're in your mom's room," Paula assured them. "We'll go say hello in just a minute." But Cal surprised her by coming around the corner of the corridor. He swung both boys into his arms and carried them over to the nursery window.

"There is your sister," he announced, his voice sounding oddly hoarse. "She's the pretty baby in the middle."

"I see her!" they shouted in unison.

Kate and John stepped closer, but Paula had to reach for her tissue again. She didn't want to look like a mess when she saw her daughter.

"Addie's okay?" she asked her son-in-law.

"She's doing great. Go see for yourself," Cal said. "I'll handle the boys."

"Thanks." She hesitated, taking another long look at the gorgeous infant behind the glass. "Oh, I almost forgot. Have you and Addie decided what you're going to call her yet?"

His smile just about took her breath away. "Valentine," Cal replied. "What else?"

Blaze™

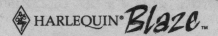

HARLEQUIN® *Blaze*™

In Harlequin Blaze, it's always

GOOD TO BE BAD

Don't miss

Debbi Rawlins's

latest sexy, red-hot read
available November 2004!

When Laurel and Rob are reunited in
GOOD TO BE BAD, sparks fly. They can't turn back,
nor can they turn away…and when an explosive secret
comes to light at their desert dig site, the temperature
isn't the only thing that's hot, hot, hot!

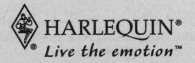

HARLEQUIN®
Live the emotion™